The Child

The Child

Kjersti A. Skomsvold

Translated from the Norwegian
by Martin Aitken

GRANTA

Granta Publications, 12 Addison Avenue, London W11 4QR

First published in Great Britain by Granta Books, 2021

Originally published in 2018 as *Barnet* by Forlaget Oktober, AS, Oslo

Published by agreement with the Oslo Literary Agency

<<translation funding to be added at proof>>

A CIP catalogue record for this book
is available from the British Library

2   4   6   8   9   7   5   3   1

ISBN 978 1 78378 546 9
eISBN 978 1 78378 548 3

www.granta.com

Typeset in Baskerville by Patty Rennie

Printed and bound by CPI Group (UK) Ltd,
Croydon, CR0 4YY

The Child

It was a new year, a new beginning, and outside the first rain was falling. It felt like a belt tightened around my waist, loosened, then tightened again, all through the night, through the morning, through the day. The rain washed the snow away and the next night I awoke as if by ambush. A thrusting pain in my back, someone punching as I slept, so hard it brought me to my knees, as if I wasn't there already.

Bo went out in the morning and came back from the bakery with a sixty-kroner loaf. I had no idea bread could be that expensive, he said, but if there was ever a time we deserved it I guess it's now. I held on and held on, soaking up the punches, the minutes ticking, the hours ticking, and there was the moon again, but I didn't want to go yet. Normally I worried about being late, now about being early. They'd said not to

3

come too early. The sounds inside my body, as if from a tortured animal, escaped from between my lips as the pain gripped me tighter.

I clung to the light of the moon, barely able to stand, let alone put one foot in front of the other. Eventually I realised that if I didn't go now I wouldn't be able to go at all.

I vomited in the taxi, vomited in the waiting room, but all the time I was in the woods, my thoughts beneath a tree, looking up into the branches. Pain tore me up; without pain I was nothing. I had no idea such pain could exist on earth, in heaven, that something inside me could hurt so much. In my pain I resided. But it was a pain I could not withstand, a pain that could never be kissed better, a pain that held me in its command. I could do nothing.

The midwife snapped at me in the delivery room. Screaming's not going to help, she said; it was about the only thing she said to me. I lost heart then, because what else could help? I'm useless when people are angry, and anyway it wasn't me; the scream was torn from my throat. I knew I wasn't going to cope, there was no way I could handle it. But then the woods appeared again. As a new surge of pain racked my body, my thoughts took me away into the woods to stand under my tree and everything around me was bright green, everywhere around me, under and over, please let it soon be over.

The new midwife was kind and considerate, she asked if it was all right for them to stick this thing inside me, to empty me out, and I said do what you want, just make it stop. She said your baby's got hair, feel, your baby's got hair, urging me to be a part of something I wanted nothing to do with. I said no, I daren't, but she took hold of my hand and guided me. I felt the baby's head, felt its hair, and that was when I understood that a living baby, an actual human being, was going to come out of me.

She heaved at her end and I heaved at mine, we were at each end of a rope, a homespun rope she'd made out of bedsheets with a knot at each end, and now we were heaving with all our might. The white rope was what rescued me, the midwife in white my human saviour, and I heaved with my arms, braced with my legs, the midwife, me and my uterus pressing and pulling and squeezing and straining, extracting the baby, the life and the heavens from my body. The pain was gone in an instant, like a balloon slipping from the hand of a child and drifting away into the clouds.

*

You're a week old now. Outside the window the first rays of morning are pale and thin; I sense your smell, and bending my head I kiss your scalp. You're asleep in your baby carrier, your face against my chest, while I write standing up, words on sticky notes I put on the bedroom wall in front of me, words on the laptop I've placed on a shelf where I stand with you cradled at my tummy, swaying from side to side. In the daytime I must carry you, at night I'm your mattress; I've tried to trick you, putting you in your own bed with a hot-water bottle and clothing that smells of me, but you find me out every time, and then you cry.

*

After the birth I wanted Bo to be there, I wanted him not to have to go home. Night settled around me in the white room, and the transparent Perspex box stood next to my bed. I opened my eyes and turned my head, and the box was still there. I closed my eyes, opened them, and yes, it was there, the baby inside it. It seemed so unreal, that I had my own child, in a Perspex box at my bedside.

I lay awake, and when I closed my eyes images flashed in front of me, my brain uncoupling for want of sleep, the most absurd images, the brightest of colours. I didn't dare have the baby in bed with me when these images came. And what if I actually did fall sleep, what then? It's bad enough sleeping on my own, with my own body; when I wake up, the parts of me I've been lying on are totally numb.

Morning came and left us bare to the world. Mostly I was scared someone would come into the room; it felt as if anyone who opened the door would see how ripped apart I was, how cut to shreds, inside and out.

7

I'd dreamt of the first milk, only now I didn't dare look down, it was like I was on a cliff with vertigo and could fall at any moment, too frightened to look and see if the milk was there, because what if it wasn't? That scared me even more than falling off a cliff, the thought of not being able to nourish my baby. Its little body was so warm, but I couldn't open the window in the boiling hot room, for the winter was out there, and all the dead besides. I felt the fear of being left on my own, felt it even though I now had a family, the terror of ending up alone.

*

You grizzle, cradled there at my tummy, unsettled. You've already caught a cold. We couldn't even protect you for a week. I'm worried you'll stop breathing, but of course you don't, children don't just stop breathing, I tell myself, although now I know it's not true. Perhaps it's wrong of me to be writing while you're still so little. A person becomes so distant when they're writing. Shouldn't I only be talking to you, smiling at you, looking after you?

8

*

I'm useless when it comes to looking after things. I ruin everything, especially the things I treasure most. There was a wall that hadn't dried and I got paint on the sleeve of my new blue coat, the old vase Edel gave me is in bits, everything I own comes apart in front of my eyes. I'm spilt, a glass of milk dropped on the floor. Giving birth to a child is a form of decay: the skeleton rattles, the pelvis comes loose, the body tears, all as if to remind me that I'm to crumble and turn to dust. *The bird fights its way out of the egg. The egg is the world. Whoever wants to be born must destroy a world.*

*

The broken women shuffled quietly about in the hospital corridors, on their way to the pharmacy for more painkillers, or to the canteen to eat. Such small steps they took, one foot gingerly in front of the other, for it hurt so much to walk, in their great big old-men's nappies, with their big, empty tummies that looked like they didn't know the babies inside them were gone, that they weren't there any more and lay now instead in their transparent Perspex boxes, which the mothers wheeled in front of them like walking aids, supporting themselves as they moved through the corridors. Their breasts were open wounds, bleeding, and the women prayed quietly for the milk to come, please let the milk come soon, please.

*

Home again, I lay awake crying over the trauma I'd been through. Is it OK to call something a trauma when it's your own doing? Whatever it was, it left me hopeless and helpless. But I couldn't lie like that for long, because then there'd be someone else crying, someone who needed me.

I placed my hand like a protective shell around the soft head, the child was a peaceful apostle. My finger was as long as the child's forearm, and his vulnerability overshadowed my own. His gaze felt like he'd already seen everything, knew everything, and was familiar with swathes of eternity. And his palm lines

10

had lint in them, the lines of his tiny hands were so deep that lint collected in them.

Illness crept in. The thought that I might get ill again is with me constantly, ready to assail me when the body is worn thin. I was worn thin after the birth, days without sleep, and what if the illness came back? If it did, we wouldn't be able to cope. We'd have to move in with my dad, I said to Bo, we wouldn't be able to cope on our own. We're not moving any-where, he said. I fed the child, as Bo fed me, and then he said we could sleep on the sofa together that night, all three of us, because then the pressure to sleep wouldn't be as great.

I dreamt that I died, I dreamt that my birthmarks bled and came away, falling from me like tired leaves from trees, and when I woke up I had to go and check in the mirror. The days then were a dance between joy and sorrow, sorrow and fear, and within the fear was the terror of going mad.

*

It can't be that bad, surely? you might be thinking now. And you'd be right, of course. It's your brother I've been talking about, by the way – when I've been telling you about the baby, the child, I've been talking about your brother, because you've got an older brother. I don't know if you can remember, but someone spat on you when you were only a few hours old. That was him. He spat on you at the hospital, but since we came home he gives you kisses and has hardly hit you at all.

I've had two children in the space of eighteen months, and now I'm not so slow any more; I was slow for thirty-four years, but in the last three everything's been going so fast. Falling in love went so fast, then being a family, of three, and then four, went even faster. Only my writing has gone so very slowly.

*

Spring came and your father and I put that first harsh winter we'd been together behind us. We sat on a bench in Peggy Guggenheim's garden, Venetian light smarted in our eyes, penetrating our thoughts, penetrating our skin. It was as if we melted together there on that bench, thawing out. The words, hidden away inside my mouth, came loose and rolled onto my tongue, those impossible words suddenly became possible. Bo said he'd been thinking the same thing. A child.

I looked at the art Peggy Guggenheim had collected, and I was afraid the artists had taken advantage of her. She seemed such a lost soul, her odd gesticulations, the way her tongue darted in and out of her mouth, but surely there was no reason to feel sorry for Peggy Guggenheim? She took advantage of the artists too: she bought their work for next to nothing, they couldn't afford to say no. She slept with the artists, or the artists slept with her, and she slept with writers too. For four days and nights she made love with the finest of them all, and presumably Samuel Beckett would only have wanted to make love for four days and nights with someone out of the ordinary? But I worry far too much about such things; why do I have to take it all so seriously, why do I have to be so afraid of allowing others to get close to me?

We travelled such a lot that spring. It was as if there were all sorts of places we had to visit so we could make a child, as if we had to try out different cities to see where we could make the child we wanted, or else we were looking for the seed of our child outside ourselves, as if the child were something we could find if only we went to the right place. And so we went to New York.

I'm no good at recounting travels, the impressions are always too many, my head's a chaos, so instead I'll tell you about when we left New York, or were about to leave. We ought to have been in the taxi that was waiting outside to take us to the airport, but all at once it came to me that at that very moment our child would be conceived. Bo put the sheet back on the bed, the sheet we'd only just tossed in the laundry basket, and then when we were sitting in the taxi afterwards I felt life streaming into me, continuing to stream into me. I felt I needed something to eat then, and at the airport I bought a sandwich, one of those revolting great cardboardy ones you get at airports, and I thought to myself how sad that the first nourishment I would give

14

to what would become our child was such an awful sandwich.

*

I need breakfast. I lift you out of your carrier so you won't get crumbs and jam in your hair. You're three weeks old now and the leaves haven't yet fallen from the trees – they cling to their twigs this autumn. I put you down on the kitchen counter. You curl upwards, embracing yourself, your face going through a repertoire of grimaces before you're properly awake, before you look around and look at me. You stretch out your frog's legs, your long frame. You're so long, it's as if you belong to other people altogether – neither Bo, nor your brother nor I myself are particularly tall. You lie there with your arms stretched over your head, as if relaxing on a lounger in the sun, while I eat a slice of bread. I haven't bathed you yet, only washed you with a cloth; in that way you still belong to the inside of me.

*

I discovered an artist on our travels, Agnes Martin. She made me feel cheerful, full of vitality, even; her simple brush strokes gave me space to think between the lines. I thought about having a child – how would I write if we had a child? We were standing in a circular room filled with her work in San Francisco. Bo told me how he used to sing in a choir when he was a boy. The conductor had polio and would limp about in the same square metre of space. His limp was probably never more conspicuous, and never less so either, for he was free, quite free inside his little square, and the same was true of Agnes Martin inside the squares she painted.

What touched me most were her words. *I've been born again and again. A hundred times I've been married. I've had hundreds of children. This time I asked to be by myself,* she said. That sentence felt like a gunshot to my head. She'd asked to be by herself in this life, and as I fixed my own life in sentences, she had fixed hers in brush strokes and grids of colour. I was her, I knew what it was like, the compulsion to fix my life in something of my own creation. I know all too well what it's like feeling you've got to work away at some eternal

16

problem, because the alternative is a restlessness that can't be managed. I need the problem to be something of my own design, a problem whose solution I can then set myself to find, even if the most important thing about the problem is that no solution exists. I've tried the opposite: sat for hours on end counting the planets and stars, and felt great satisfaction in knowing that I would arrive at an answer if only I kept at it long enough. I loved to be clever, but then it was never sufficient.

Agnes Martin left New York, where she was friends with some of the greatest artists, and for a year she was just gone, no one knew where she was, until she surfaced again in no-man's land. In the desert of New Mexico she built her own house, and after seven years of silence she started creating art again. She didn't read the newspapers, and ate only bananas. She painted with her back to the world. Hundreds of husbands, hundreds of children – please don't give me any more, she said. I wanted to write with my back to the world too. I was scared stiff of doing anything else, and I could have done what she did: I could have asked God

17

to be by myself. But then again, this one life is all I've got.

The last work Agnes Martin completed before her death was a drawing on a small sheet of paper, only ten centimetres high It's quite unlike the work for which she is known: no grids, no straight lines; her lines here have got out of control, have become crumpled and clumsy-looking. The picture resembles a flower drawn by a child. It's as if her hand has taken over from her will, life has taken over just before death – it could no longer be contained in such a stringent framework. It was no use asking God to be left by herself; in the end it was she who had to detach.   .

*

I woke at four in the morning needing to pee. I'd read that the truth lies in the first urine of the day, that it collects during the night and reveals itself when morning comes. It's the same with writing: the truth is there before the strongest light of day. But outside

it was pitch dark and I didn't know how I was going
to cope with such a momentous piece of information
while still tender and steeped in the night. I knew
I had to save the truth until I was ready, so I crept
out of the bedroom and found a plastic container in
the kitchen cabinet and peed in it, before putting it
in a carrier bag which I then tucked away inside a
shoulder bag.

I went back to bed and lay there awake, thinking of
the Russian dolls I had when I was little. I liked the
smallest one best, the one that was innermost and
couldn't be taken apart, as small as a grain of rice.
How they'd managed to paint something so small I
couldn't fathom. I couldn't go back to sleep, because
if Bo woke up before me he might find the container,
even though I'd hidden it well, and he'd wonder
what was in it and then be sorry when he opened it
and looked.

So I got up and unwrapped the truth again. Some
seconds passed, a whole life, and then, at last, a
thin violet stripe appeared in the little window, and
another. When I woke Bo up and told him he seemed

quite astonished, he couldn't get a word out, despite the fact we'd been planning for this and he knew it could happen.

We went out like we were brand new. I kept thinking that everyone could surely see the thin violet stripes we carried, which divided our lives into two, because now nothing would ever be the same again. We stopped in the bookshop and bought a book about pregnancy as if to celebrate. We were raring to go. I opened the book. *The weeks that follow are the riskiest of all*, it said. *Brace yourself.* I fell apart completely.

*

I kept waking up, distraught and without a bump. On those mornings the world felt so very dangerous. I thought I had to *will* my tummy to get bigger; I put my all into it, but there was nothing to see. Maybe I'd been imagining things?

I went for a walk with a girfriend in the park and saw the scorch mark in the grass where a man had set himself on fire a few weeks earlier. I was there when it happened. I'd never seen a dead person before, and I didn't realise at first that it even was a person – someone had covered him, and under the white cover it was as if there were two sticks pointing up. But then when they took the cover away I saw him. I saw then that it was a human being. He was lying on his back with his arms outstretched, as if he were trying to catch a bird in his bare hands, only there were no birds, just a blue, blue sky. I wondered what it was he'd been reaching for. I walked home again, full and empty at the same time, like after a funeral, and I thought about what it was I had buried there as I stood and watched, why I'd stood there for so long.

Passing the scorch mark with my friend, I found myself again wondering who he was and why he'd chosen such a violent and painful death surrounded by other people, why hadn't he hanged himself in the shower instead. Was the man in the park trying to tell us something? I had no idea what it might be. It's as if there are no limits here in the world, no limits to what can happen to us, the things we can do to ourselves.

My friend asked if I was pregnant – did it show already? I wasn't yet ready to tell anyone, and didn't know what to say; the scorched grass made it even harder. But I had to say something. It felt as if the child left me when I said yes, as if I were trying to make something real that wasn't quite real yet. I felt so cold, though the sun was out and there was no wind. My friend lent me her shawl to put over my shoulders, but it didn't help. I clutched my abdomen, afraid I'd already lost it.

When I got home Bo asked what the matter was, but I didn't tell him about the child. I told him about the scorch mark in the park, the way people had been sitting about with their disposable barbecues, how grotesque it was. A wasp buzzed noisily, bumping against the pane, unable to find its way out into the summer, and I came apart in sadness. The child will live or the child will die, Bo said to comfort me. That's how it is.

*

Now you're the one who's hungry. I feel it in my body, the milk bursting to be out, and you wake up and begin to cry. It nearly always happens in that order, as if we share the same body. But first you need changing, you've pooed up your back, which is covered in downy hair – you've dark downy hair on your back, your tummy, your legs, like a little creature found under some sticks in the wood. I put you face down on the changing table, and there you become a little chick pecking at seeds, your head wobbling up and down, searching for food. You cry from hunger, but just as we've sat down in the chair and you're about to tuck in, to suck the warm milk inside you, you discover the sun outside the window – it looks like a lamp glowing in the grey sky. You fall silent, stare and stare.

*

We were a family now. We went on our summer holidays together, Bo and I, and the little seed inside my tummy. There was a lowest common multiple; your brother had started peeing inside me and I no longer

23

needed to will him into being. But I hadn't been on a proper holiday in ten years – all I ever did was write, and it was alarming not to feel the keyboard under my fingertips.

We stayed in the summer house that had belonged to Bo's great-grandmother, a lovely place with forest on one side and the fjord on the other. I'm no good at staying in other people's houses. If I start the dishwasher I worry that the colour will wash off the plates, if I start the washing machine I worry that it's going to leak, I can't open the patio door without being concerned that I might not be able to close it again, and if I can't close the patio door it means I can't leave the place, because you can't walk away from other people's houses if there's a door left open. I don't actually think any of this is going to happen – of course not – but I can't stop myself from thinking that it *might*.

It was night and I lay sleepless. Bo was well away; he slept soundly every night and still does. Every night when he went to bed he'd be thinking about plasterboard; he made art out of plasterboard, and

24

every night he would fall asleep immediately. Now he thinks more about other things, but I've stopped asking what.

Falling asleep doesn't happen to me. But I have to, of course, and so I must strive for sleep, even if I know that the more I strive, the more elusive it becomes. Sometimes I wonder if I actually sleep at all, if I ever have. When I do, if that's what I do, it feels like I'm still awake, watching over the person who sleeps. I wonder if she hurts anywhere, I wonder if she might be hungry, if her nose is blocked, if she's left the hob on, if there's even the slightest reason for her not to be sleeping at that moment.

I woke Bo, and he said that if I couldn't sleep then he wouldn't either. Think what a time we'd have together if neither of us slept! I wondered then if he was mad.

But then he got scared, scared that perhaps I was mad; I was so out of myself with despair that it seemed as if I was. When I can't sleep I imagine all the terrible things that can happen – I might become confined to bed again the way I was when I was ill, and isn't there a thing called sleep-deprivation breakdown? I'm afraid of not being able to do anything the next day, of not being able to take part in things, because I want to run, to swim in the lake and to write. What if someone expects me to do something or go somewhere with them and I can't because I haven't slept? Besides, my thoughts are so dark when I lie awake at night, and I fear those thoughts, because I'm not sure if they're actually my thoughts, or if it's the night playing tricks on me.

But surely there's no reason to be *that* despairing? Bo said, despite all these good reasons. And just as he said it he became scared in the darkness. He thought it was his great-grandmother, who left her husband and children to be an artist in Paris, who wouldn't let us sleep and wanted to talk to us, that it was she who was keeping us awake. I understood then that I couldn't keep bothering him like that with my sleeplessness.

I wake him only seldom now, but sometimes I place his limp, sleeping hand on my head for comfort. I think the hardest thing is trying to relate to all the others, those who sleep at night. There's a light in front of their faces, they can see ahead into the new day and look forward to it coming, whereas I have the dark and sleepless night behind me like a shadow and am dreading the next one already. I don't think our two worlds have anything in common.

*

I've put you back in your baby carrier again, only then in a fit of coughing you throw up all the milk, vomiting over both of us. You're six weeks old and still you cough; I don't know if it's the old cough or a new one. How can so much milk find room in a tummy the size of a pea? It can't have been true what the midwife told us, she must have been lying.

*

After we came home from the summer house I went up to Lofoten on my own to write. It was the first

27

time in six months I'd done something without Bo; we'd been together every second, getting used to each other.

I went to Lofoten to write, but all I did was read. I sat in what was once a fisherman's cabin reading, not noticing when evening came, the daylight continuing through the night. In the daytime I cycled about beneath the fells, on those scattered islands that seem to be trying to get away from the rest of the country. Eagles flew above me, their legs dangling down, and the peaks tore at the sky. My tummy was beginning to bulge, and I thought about who the person inside me was. Sometimes I thought I heard a child's laughter, but when I turned to look it was only the wind. I didn't feel sick, and the strong smell of the fish hung out to dry all around didn't bother me. Mum cycled about Lofoten too when she was pregnant with me, and she says it caused quite a stir, for she was five or six months gone and very big. She'd stood on the ferry with her bike and her big tummy, trying to dry her clothes in the wind because it had rained so much.

The last day I was there, I saw orcas inside the fjord. I got off my bike and stood there watching them; I wasn't alone. I thought about the homeless person I'd seen in a documentary, who one night broke into SeaWorld in America, took off his clothes and jumped into the tank. They found him dead the next day, draped over the back of the biggest of their captive orcas, naked, his testicles mangled. I would never have imagined that such a thing could happen.

The enormous whales in the fjord dived and reappeared by turns, as if they were putting on a show. I sensed they knew I was watching them and felt grateful they were showing off for me instead of staying underwater, when that was safest for them. I know they split up into groups when people go out in boats to catch them; the males swim in one direction, the mothers and the young in another. The whales don't want humans to take their babies, so they try to distract them, to make them follow the males instead. The saddest part of the documentary was when the baby whales were taken from their parents, the way the mothers sang their grief, vocalising at the lowest of frequencies, in the hope that their babies, wherever they were, would hear them.

Outside the café serving fishcakes I sat and lingered with dried fish heads dangling above me, big as beach balls. Their eyes looked as if they'd been drawn and stuck on, pale irises and dark pupils, quite vacant. Some of the mouths were gaping, as if still in astonishment at having swallowed the lure, being hauled up through the water, suddenly having to gulp air against their will, until the crack on the head when the bright sky so abruptly turned into darkness. Small birds pecked at the bread crumbs I tossed them, then fluttered into the air to hop about inside the fish heads like my own compulsive thoughts.

My index finger drew the outline of the fells around me; they looked like heartbeats captured by a machine. I thought of the enormous forces that had been unleashed when the ice retreated, how it had shoved and barged the fells about, and yet it was the fells which had remained, the oldest things in the world. I biked on, feeling my debt to what I'd seen, knowing I had to write.

*

August Strindberg fled from the world. He pretended he'd been unfaithful so he could get away from his wife and write. He needed to be on his own in order to *purify his individuality and refine his spirit.* He was so yielding, so accommodating of those around him, fearful that he should be considered ungrateful, and I, likewise, am too yielding, too grateful by far, apart from when I'm with Bo.

When your brother was born I got it into my head that my brain must have been altered, that it must have changed colour and shape, and that accordingly the thoughts that came out through my hand should be different too. I imagined I'd soon begin to access a whole new language, that I would be able to submerge myself in a part of me I hadn't been in touch with before, and at night when I lay awake with him I would use this new language to write words and sentences whose like the world had not yet seen.

But it wasn't the child that altered my brain, coloured and shaped it anew: it was the experience of going

31

through a crisis. And this didn't change the words, it stole them, and no new ones came to me at all. The only thing I managed to write was that I was crying. I'm crying, crying all the time, I wrote.

*

So it feels even more crucial to be writing now. I wake up in the mornings and look at you and say, today we must work, little one! It was as if you had to come, as if I had to have you to tell you all these things, you had to come and create another new beginning so that I could see in some reasonably clear light the years that went before, and see the change that has taken place.

Only three years ago I sat alone in my flat, writing my way through the days, the nights, the seasons, eating the same food, alternating between chicken sausages and salmon fillet, doing my shopping in the nearest corner shop, thinking I didn't have time to go to the supermarket only a couple of minutes further down the road; it was so hard for me to consider all the time I wasted doing things other than writing.

Now I'm writing as I stand here. On the shelf next to the laptop is a half-eaten slice of bread and liver pâté – what's left of your brother's breakfast; he handed it to me when he and Bo left home this morning. On top of the slice of bread is a pink dummy, which you spit out every time I put it in your mouth, and next to the bread a bunch of keys, found perhaps by your brother on his way home from nursery school. I live now in a flat full of little towers of other people's childhoods. Life can change so completely.

*

I felt I was passing on my sadness to what was living inside me even before it was born. It didn't matter how happy I was about everything that had happened (and to think that *this* had happened too – a baby!), I felt I was passing on my depression to the child every single day. Whenever my sadness welled up, I was certain it seeped through into this new person too. I thought about the deepest darkness in which the child lay, and there I was, making it even darker with all my miserable thoughts.

*

But then the most miraculous things began to happen. Autumn came. We heard the heart that beat beneath my own.

*

The nights wore me out. I don't think it was the baby waking me up, I think I was awake already, and the baby would wake to keep me company. Hands and feet pushed at the thin skin of my abdomen, pressed against my palm, and yet it was still so hard to imagine a human being was inside me.

In the daytime these movements tagged along with me, preparing me for what was to come. The child clung to me, embraced me; instead of me carrying the child, it felt like the other way round, the child was ferrying me, and I couldn't see the world at all without seeing the child. I went to the botanical gardens, thinking it was safe there. There were prams and pushchairs all around, mums and dads and all these little sleeping people being pushed about.

Then one day it was Bo I saw all of a sudden, walking behind a pram. I stopped, rooted to the spot, my heart thumping as if it would leap from the cage of my chest as I observed him together with a family that wasn't ours. But it wasn't him after all. It took a long time for the nausea I felt to recede, for my heart to beat normally again. I'm sorry, I whispered to the child, I was seeing things, that's all. I'm sorry.

I thought I'd calmed down, but just before we got home a man came towards me with something distorting his face. I had to turn and hurry away in the opposite direction. Then I almost bumped into a young woman; she took her hand out of her pocket and ran it swiftly over the sharp blade she then thrust into my stomach, and I didn't know if it was her blood or mine that was staining the pavement. I started to run, my eyes fixed on the ground; please, I prayed, please let the child survive, even if I don't.

*

And you, you were content inside me. I was able to surrender to you the responsibility of staying alive. In the daytime, having another small child to run about after, I barely had time to think about you there, but in the evenings I would talk to you, check to make sure there were still signs of life, which there were. I used to think it was scary having children inside me, the fact that I couldn't see you, but in many ways it's scarier when they come out, because anything can happen then – they can go blue in the face and lie lifeless on the floor. These things can happen in the womb too, I suppose, only you can't see it then.

Maybe it was easier being pregnant with you because it was my second time, but I wonder too if having a girl inside you is different to having a boy. I was so fragile with your brother inside me, whereas I thought I needed to be strong for you, because I didn't want you to be as feeble as me, someone who takes the blame for everything instead of thinking it could be someone else who was wrong. I wanted you to know that it's often other people who are wrong.

When I was pregnant the first time, Bo couldn't see himself having a son; he knew, and knows, so many difficult males. As a child he never liked doing what the other boys did, and still doesn't – the sort of things I like, such as running and playing football. Now, as ever, he prefers to sit on his own in a corner, to hide away in a bush, as it were, and even in such a quiet, out-of-the-way place the world can still be overwhelming. He could see himself as father to a girl, but not at all to a boy, and this worried him. I was unable to raise his spirits when he thought about it; it didn't matter what I said, nothing helped.

But then one day he phoned me and he was so joyful – he told me he'd just been to the supermarket. He'd gone there from the studio without getting changed, and behind him in the checkout queue there was a little boy who kept looking up at him and staring at his trousers before eventually turning to his mother

37

and whispering to her, as if it were the craziest thing he'd ever seen: that man's got paint on his trousers. And that was when Bo realised he'd quite like a son after all.

*

I put the child in the horrid pram. I didn't want to think about all the things that could happen, but I couldn't stop myself. I imagined how every car that came towards us would swerve onto the pavement and mow us down, and I gripped the handle as if my treacherous hands might otherwise let go at any moment. I didn't know how to carry myself – my spine was at a loss without my heavy stomach in front of it. Everything was out of balance, as if my body could no longer centre, and my thoughts were the same, they couldn't centre either, there was nowhere they could find rest.

In the shops and cafés I noticed all the other spidery bodies with their bulging abdomens and gangly legs, even more so than when I'd been pregnant myself.

I thought of what they would soon have to endure and felt sorry for them. But I couldn't say anything – it was too late now, there was nothing they could do about it, and so all I did was smile and nod and carry on.

I zigzagged through the cemetery, looking for names for the child. Names on headstones are more alive than names in books or names on doorbells; it's easier to see the people behind them, the lives they lived. Birds were gathered in the trees above me, dark little blobs on the branches, like chirping afflictions, and I could almost hear illness whisper in the distance then, making ready to swipe us off our feet. I stared at the gravestones in their criss-crossing rows, the way they tipped like rotten teeth in an old and decrepit jaw. Even after death we cannot overcome nature.

It didn't stop when I got home. What if I threw the child out of the window or off the balcony outside? I didn't, but what if I did? And so I hadn't the nerve to open the window or go out onto the balcony, but stood in the middle of the living room, clinging to that little body.

Can we bolt the balcony door shut, and the windows? But Bo didn't understand what I was saying; I was stammering, I'd lost my language, the sentences wouldn't come out of my mouth.

Dear God, I prayed. Don't let me lose my joy.

Lack of sleep removed me from the world. Night came, if darkness is night, and then the light outside returned, without me seeing light at all; when you wake up without having slept, not even birdsong can gladden you. Before I knew it, it was morning, a new day, only I'd ruined it before it even began. I wouldn't ever be as good for the child as I wanted to be, the way I would have been if I'd been able to sleep, and I couldn't sleep in the daytime; sleeping in the daytime is one of the loneliest things I know.

*

Now I can bring myself to think I'm good enough most of the time, even if I haven't slept; you'll have

40

to take me as I am, my little one. It's morning and you're two months old. I sense that you're in love with me, infatuated almost; you light up when I look at you, then look away again coyly. And I'm in love with you too. You smooth your tiny hand gently over my arm, and I feel flattered that you care for me. You're imposing slightly higher demands on our conversations now and become offended if I don't respond, you stop smiling. I think it's a good sign.

*

The thing I promised myself wasn't going to happen happened, and I thought that Bo and I were ruining the child by arguing in front of him. I can't remember what it was we argued about, but I think perhaps it was the morning I got up to take the dog out and Bo asked if I could buy some loo paper while I was at it. It was an innocent enough request, I can see that now, but at the time it felt like something quite unmanageable. I couldn't handle the idea that the child might get hungry while I was out, that the dog had to be taken for a walk, that we needed loo paper,

41

that there were other people I had to deal with – all these things at once. Or maybe it was the time Bo was going to text his former partner – not the last one, but the one before that. We'd found a name for the child, only then it felt a bit odd because his former partner also had a child with the same name, he said, and he thought it best to inform her from the start. I can understand that now, in hindsight, but at the time it felt like the name broke and came apart, and I was distraught.

Or maybe it was just me saying something stupid, but whatever it was we argued about, all of a sudden it had happened, the child had heard us, and even if he didn't seem that bothered, it must have affected him, changed him in some way, made his nervous system that little bit different to how it was before. I wondered how many kisses, how many cuddles, it would take to repair him, and if we could live long enough to give him and each other sufficient love to make it right.

*

Perhaps I'm trying, consciously or not, to heal the wounds inflicted in my first family, my childhood family? Perhaps that's why it's doubly painful when new wounds come, because they're not really new wounds, but old, underlying wounds opening up again.

The strange thing is that I hardly knew those wounds existed before I had a family of my own. Now I hear my mother in myself, my mother going round the house crying, without anyone knowing why, and I hear my father's sighs in Bo's sighs. I always thought Mum cried too much, like a child almost, but now I do the same. It's never anything trivial at the time, but something much bigger, and how can we stay together if we can't talk? Dad would just go quiet, and now Bo carries that same silence. I try to put on a new face instead of this weeping-clown mask, but I'm so distraught, and I can't understand why Bo can't just give me a hug, because a hug's all I need, surely? Instead we lose our way, stumbling headlong into fright, which turns into anger, and we find ourselves in a labyrinth it takes an eternity to get out of again. Such a long time it takes for everything to subside, for the anger to turn into grief at our not having managed to be better.

I told Bo about the wounds. I asked him if he thought that was what it was. And then he told me a story about his grandfather, about how they came to burn the apple trees his grandfather had nurtured, the trees he'd nurtured for forty years, which were sick. But Bo's grandfather was cunning: he made an incision in the big apple tree in front of the house, into which he grafted a mistletoe. Trees with mistletoe in them are protected by law, so they couldn't take his last apple tree, and in that way the genealogy of his trees was safe.

In the wounds we inflict on each other (or perhaps it's the same wound that just gets a bit bigger, a bit deeper every time) we have planted a child, two children, and from these wounds our children will grow.

*

Giving birth was much easier second time round, mostly because the staff were nice and had plenty of time. It was a different ward, with bean-bags and candles, and you were born in a tub of warm water. I'm not going to pretend it was pleasant, though, because I was in terrible pain in that tub. I threw up over the edge, the pain gathering like a storm just as it had the first time, and I told myself I wasn't ever going to pretend to anyone it had been pleasant. What helped was the midwife not getting annoyed at how hopeless I was, but saying considerately to Bo: it's the pain that's making her vomit now. I screamed, because it helps to scream, and then you emerged, a furious little thing who screamed almost as loudly as me.

Before my first time someone I knew said: You can look forward to it! But I needn't have bothered. I'll never be able to go through that again, I told myself afterwards, it was such a horrendous experience. But then the second time cancelled it out, and now it's hard for me to think I might never give birth again. The second time, I just knew I was going to split open, knew I was going to bleed and die, that I'd

45

never be the same person again once I got through to the other side. But at least I knew there *was* another side – I hadn't thought there would be the first time. I wish I could have one more chance to feel the whole world, the whole of the future and the past, come together like that in a little room, together with a brand-new human being.

*

You're a calmness that has come into the flat – your breath, your warmth – and even though things can still be chaotic here, I wonder what on earth we were doing the first time around, the way we went about things. Of course I shouldn't wonder at all; mothers with more than one child have no business pretending to know better. I can't be the judge of the person I was when I'd only just given birth to my first baby; a first-time mother is so totally in the hands of nature. It physically hurt if someone else held the child, touched him with hands that might not be clean. It hurt when I couldn't be sure if they were supporting his head properly, or when their voices were too loud, and it was as if the bottom fell out of me if he cried and someone else tried to comfort him. I wanted to snatch the child from their arms then and hide away in a dark room, with other dark rooms around it. Dark and empty, room upon room, one inside the other, and outside there'd be a forest so vast it covered the entire globe and blanketed everything with its silence and tranquility. And then, once I started to think that now we were safe and no one could ever find us ever again, then I'd be able to start breathing.

*

Come and see! Bo calls out, and then again. I dash into the living room and see him lying on the sofa with the child lying on his chest, whether it's you or your brother when he was smaller. The child lifts its head, like a cobra, and it looks like the head is coming out of Bo's chest.

When Bo had finished his first year at school the teacher asked him what he'd learned. Bo thought for a moment and said: I learned to draw a flower. At parents' evening the teacher said: He seems to be making progress with the alphabet. But Bo had been able to read and write for at least a couple of years already, only no one at the school had realised.

Maybe that's why he sees even the smallest steps in the child's development. He says now that the child has discovered its feet, the child is rubbing its feet together like an insect, as if massaging its soles and making them ready to walk. Bo sees different things from me. To me it's as if the child's movements are my movements. At night I feel them in my body as if I've been on a boat all day and the ground rises and falls like the sea underneath me even when I'm back on land.

I've noticed too that I'm much more patient than I thought. I've never had patience, apart from in my writing, but with you and your brother, I'm patience itself. It was a big worry for me before the two of you were born, much less so now. I can sing for you for hours on end. The child wakes up as if from a night-mare, and of course he can't tell me what he dreamt, so I sing him to sleep again. He lies in my arms and gazes up at the ceiling as I sing.

I'm better at looking after you than I am at looking after the dog, and I'm better at looking after the dog than I am at looking after the peace lily I bought. The peace lily has withered and the dog's having to stay with my dad. She's got a sore on her head that won't heal, and I think it's because I haven't been able to look after her properly. I haven't been able to pay her enough attention, take her on long enough walks, and all of these things came out in that sore. I'm on my own with the dog, because even though it was Bo who said she could sleep in our room at night, he won't ever get used to living with a dog. His movements in her presence are just as unnatural and inhibited as when we first got together. He reminds me of when I was little and my girlfriend had a parrot that used to fly around the living room. I was scared stiff every time it landed on my head, too scared to move or even say a word, all I could do was smile gawkily. Dad's fond of the dog; she's better off with him, even if I do miss her every day.

You won't let me out of your sight. You sit there in your baby bouncer as I go about the living room, wash up in the kitchen; your eyes follow me everywhere. Your bottom lip quivers if I disappear from view, and you sigh with relief when I come back. You've realised I'm the one who's keeping you alive.

We're ill again, as we've been all autumn. I blame the nursery school. Your brother started nursery this autumn; now it's winter and we're still ill. It's as if the children turn into vagrants at nursery school – he comes home with sores on his face, lice in his hair, yellow pus in the corners of his eyes, and a cough that sounds like it belongs to another time. But he lights up as soon as he sees the other kids. Ilse, Ilse! he says, and throws his arms around little Ilse, who's dressed up as a black cat, and this makes up for everything – I can't give him what other children can. I can't wait until you're old enough to start playing with your brother, and I can't wait until summer, your first summer, then you'll know what it's like to be alive without a cough.

*

It was your brother's first summer, and we drove the old Volvo across the country to where Bo's from, to where he always longs to go back to – his great-grandmother's house. We rolled the windows down and said, We love this. We said it twice, three times, again and again. We love this.

In the daytime we went about quietly, meandering in and out of the rooms, barely even aware of each other's presence, brushing past each other in door-ways, a fleeting caress. Bo sat in a chair writing, I went down to the jetty and looked at the light shimmering above the surface of the fjord. The child was asleep in the pram, under the great copper beech. Together we walked in the woods or went swimming. Bo played with the child on his jungle mat, I picked redcurrants with the child on my arm. We were alone in time, together in time, each of us slotted into the ideas we had about how we wanted to live in time that was ours, and our ideas matched up – we didn't need to plan a thing.

It was evening, it was night, it was morning or day, and I came in to Bo. He was lying on the bed in the yellow-painted room with his eyes open, his hands stretched towards me, because it was what his hands wanted. His body stretched towards me, and I received him, because it was what my body wanted. The house was quiet and we received each other. Outside the wind was blowing.

We need daylight in our eyes, trembling air in our nostrils, and I wonder if we should go for a walk in the woods today. I miss the woods as much as I miss the dog, more even, although I never miss the dog more than when we're in the woods; I can't put it any less emotionally than that. I grew up in a loving family and we lived by the woods. Those woods, and later the feeling of missing them, live inside me now.

I think being in the woods is a bit like reading poetry. *Poetry is not a turning loose of emotion, but an escape from emotion; it is not the expression of personality, but an escape from personality. But, of course, only those who have personality and emotion know what it means to want to escape from these things.*

I used to think that what was good about the woods was that I knew who I was there, but the truth is that in the woods I am finally free of myself, I can simply exist. In my writing I decide for myself who I am, but there too it's only when I give up my protection, when I become detached from the thought of what the words are meant to be, to become, that something emerges in which I can recognise myself. It's the same with love too. In love, and in woods and poetry, I can escape from myself. Thoughts and emotions become healed.

*

I close the door of the flat and go down the long flight of stairs with you in the carrycot. The phone is in my other hand, with the voice memo app open. I click the carrycot into place on the pram, only then I don't know what to do, I don't know which direction to go. We've moved from my old flat closer to the centre of town; there's a lot more people around and I'm not getting any sleep again. When people gather in the courtyard at one in the morning and I sense what they're up to, all my shyness disappears. I lean out of the window and shout at them: You're *not* having a party here now!

I've heard banging noises from the loft, like someone rummaging around in the storage units. I think someone's sleeping up there at night. Bo says I'm imagining things, but I'm not, I hear the noises even with ear plugs. I found an empty packet of lozenges up there, and these little scraps of gold paper, which I'm sure are drug-related, but I haven't the courage to go up at night, only in the day, and there's nothing to see then.

In the place I lived as a child there were only two directions to go: to the woods or into town. Above the terrace of houses where we lived were ponds and animals, below it tower blocks rose up out of the ground. Where we live now I can go in any direction – to the cemetery and the crows, to the skyscrapers and the stockbrokers, to the river and the illegal salmon fishermen, to the shopping street where every day is market day. I can go to the park where the

Roma people sit with their disposable barbecues. The choices are many.

The woods are just that little bit too far away, out of reach – all the hills I'd have to climb to get there, the deprivation I'd have to encounter along the way, and the wealth too. I'm startled when I see the elderly beggar on the pavement; one side of his face is covered in hair, like a thick layer of fur. I stride right past him, even though I see the child in him, the way he's sleeping with his head dropped to his shoulder; what kind of a person am I?

So I go to the botanical gardens, where I dwell among trees. I like going for the same walk every day.

*

A year ago now, I sat on a bench here and looked at the dead flowers; it was your brother I held on my lap then. He was already venturing into the world, and when we were lying on the sofa together I'd have

56

to press his head against my chest to make him stay there. I didn't realise how fast everything changes, how briefly the magnolia trees are in bloom, how quickly the pinched-handkerchief bracts of the dove tree disappear. I'd sat with the child in my arms all through the spring, the summer, the autumn; he was in my arms and in my heart and all the time he was changing ever so slightly. There was something new by the minute, and something else that was lost, and before I knew it that time was gone.

What if I came to forget the way he would lie there whispering after he woke up, as if he were afraid to prick a hole in the day, or the night, with his voice? What if I came to forget the way he moved his feet when he was eating, as if he were playing the piano, stepping on its golden pedals? I knew I wouldn't be able to write everything down, and so I wrote hardly anything. My thoughts disappeared before I was able to turn them into writing, the words became as fleeting as the memories, and soon I'd forgotten it all.

Now I'm writing again, and I hope it doesn't mean that I'm missing you, I don't want to miss you. I think of Edel, at once I think of her. You never knew Edel, but perhaps it's not too late?

*

Edel was at the kitchen window waving when Bo and I arrived, the gravel crunched under our shoes as we went up to the house. Edel was my great-aunt, and she used to look after me when I was little.

The old house was locked in time, everything was exactly the same as thirty years before. The curtains in the bedroom were the same, but now they were drawn. She always used to be so particular about opening the curtains in the morning, in case the neighbours thought we were lying in. The same lugubrious glass owl sat on the windowsill staring out at passers-by, and the kick-sledge was still parked outside the front door. Once Edel would swish along with her husband on the seat in front of her; now the sledge just stood there, winter and summer alike.

Edel beamed through the window, as beautiful as ever, though she'd never much cared about her looks. For many years I didn't realise. All through my childhood it had been invisible to me that Edel would one day be gone, but then suddenly it became clear, and now it was hard to remember it had ever been any different. Every time I came to see her I was reminded that she was slipping through my fingers.

I saw that she was trying to open the window, her fingers fiddling with the catch as if she couldn't wait to greet us, couldn't wait for the moment we would step into the house. I gestured to her to come to the door instead – I pointed, then turned towards Bo: Well, come on, then; I didn't want Edel to have to stand there any longer not being able to open the window; it made her seem so helpless.

We saw our reflections in the puddle outside her door. Puddles can reflect stars too, but that didn't help. The hug I gave her was no use either. She was even smaller than the last time I'd seen her, shrinking relative to the door frame as I had once risen. Every time I was there we'd make a new pencil mark on the door frame and marvel at how much taller I was; I'd always grown so alarmingly in the meantime. How you've grown, Edel said to me now, studying me solicitously.

At the same time as she was receding from me, she had never been nearer. I thought about her even more when I didn't see her, when weeks had passed since I'd seen her last. The summer is never more compelling to us than when it's on the wane. The warm days of late August, perhaps even early September – that's when you feel the sun warming you like never before, and the mornings and afternoons spent swimming implant themselves in the body, as if to hibernate there.

I'm crossing my fingers for you, my dear, and wishing you all the very best! she said. She always spoke as if I were already on my way again, as if it were the last time we'd ever speak. Wishing me well for the future, and how glad she was that I wasn't ill any more. It won't come back, will it? she asked, her old song. You're over it now for good, aren't you? Yes, it's over now, I said. And she stroked my cheek.

I'm sorry I've not had my hair done, she said. She was always so sad about her hair. As a child, I thought she'd been born with curls, in fact I thought so even when I was grown up. Her socks had slipped down around her ankles, and her cheeks were wrinkled like the apples in the basket on the sideboard.

The peonies I put on the table didn't help. The sitting room was littered with handkerchiefs and cotton pads, and pills that had fallen on the floor. When I was little I'd played with two plastic animals on the same prickly brown carpet. Edel didn't have that many toys I could play with, but she did have an antelope and a lion, and that was why I thought she came from Africa. The animals grazed on the carpet in front of the fireplace. I had to be careful not to burn myself – my brother still has a scar over one eyebrow.

I picked up the pills and gave them to Edel, and when I did so she took my hands in her own, which were thin and cold. Her skin had become so transparent, even on the palms of her hands, that we forgave each other everything, no matter what was

61

to come. I looked at her wedding ring; it was too small for her now. Her finger seemed to have grown into it, the way a tree grows into a fence. I supposed it could have been resized, but it felt like that would be going against all the years she'd been married, as if everything then would have been in vain.

She put her hand to the wall for support as she went into the kitchen. Her legs weren't what they used to be; the last three days they'd barely been there for her at all. She'd fallen twice, once in the bathroom and once in the kitchen. I'll ask the doctor to come, I said. The last time he came, he'd asked her if she had pains in her stomach. She told him she hadn't, but then when he pressed her abdomen she'd yelped in pain. It wasn't good, what with her legs and her stomach, it wasn't good at all.

I've forgotten how to keep going, Edel said. Her not remembering meant that she was fading, further and further away from herself, away from me. Soon there'd be nothing left, everything would be erased and gone. There'd be no one there to utter her laughter, her lovely, rasping laughter; it had been put away like the silverware, hidden so well that no one was ever going to find it again. I haven't the foggiest where I've put the silverware, she said. Maybe someone stole it without me knowing?

It was her not remembering that made me remember too much, too much of what once had been. For every question she asked, I had too many answers. I remembered the person she used to be, I remembered the child in me, from a time when there was all the time in the world. I would sit on her knee, playing my favourite game; I would pretend I was her mother, without her knowing.

Edel asked us to sit on the sofa while she found us something to eat. There's no need, I told her, but it was the only thing she had left, she said, the only thing she could do.

She'd woken in the middle of the night, she told us from the kitchen, and found herself lying on the floor instead of in bed, but it was hard to work out what she made of it, because her hearing was so poor. When I asked her, she put her head round the door and said there was only one thing she wanted for her funeral, and that was proper church bells, not your recorded rubbish. Apart from that you can do as you please, she said.

She dozed off as we sat at the table with our open sandwiches, the same ones I ate when I was a child, with liver pâté that tasted of something other than liver paste. On top of the ham she still put a segment of mandarin, something we never did at home. Edel sat there dozing between Bo and me, then all of a sudden she woke up and said there was something she had to tell us. It's a bugger being old, she said. You don't want to look forward to it. No, I said, I'm not, and Bo agreed. But listen, Edel, I said, I've got something to say as well. And I told her about the child. A smile spread across her face, and she beamed. I'll have to keep going a bit, then, she said.

I pictured her with the child that was to come, imagined it making her laugh, the child discovering its laughter, and Edel rediscovering hers; it wasn't all gone yet. She'd hold the child in her arms, and the child would look back at her as if recognising her from some previous life. But she was nearly a hundred years old – the child would never remember her. If there was something I could have passed on to the child, it would have been Edel.

I asked if she needed help to go to the bathroom, but she said no, she didn't want anyone helping her on the loo. All I want is someone's hand to hold when I die, she said. But now you'd best be going.

As we stood on the step again she looked at Bo and said everyone had thought the last bus had gone as far as I was concerned, that it was too late for me to start a family, but thanks to him it wasn't too late at all. Then she looked at me and said: You're not going to be writing any more books now, are you?

*

Before I went to sleep that night, I lay thinking about Edel. I thought about Edel in black and white, the way she looked in the photo on the bookshelf when she was sixteen on a trip to the fells. She was looking out of the doorway of the cabin together with a girl-friend of hers. The person taking the photograph would later be her husband; her father only allowed her to go on the trip if her girlfriend went as well. I wondered if Edel was awake too. It felt as if I were lying next to her, the way I did when I was a child, under the big, heavy covers. I'd twirl her hair around my finger as we listened to the aeroplanes flying over the house. *Plane* was the first word I learned to say.

I thought about what it must be like to stand on the threshold of such a vast and dark eternity, what it must be like to be leaving everything – your own his-tory, all the animals, all the people.

In my dream the birds had stopped and the sky was torn open. It was the second time I'd seen a dead person. She was so small lying there. A shaft of light fell on her face. She didn't look real, but her floral-patterned blouse did, and the roses looked more rose-like than usual. She reminded me of a doll I had as a child, a plastic doll that didn't have proper doll's clothes, but a knitted sweater, knitted trousers. Edel looked like a doll too, something that wasn't real.

It was only her blouse that was real. I couldn't see if she was wearing her wedding ring. They'd folded her hands, one on top of the other, so I couldn't tell if they'd removed it, if they'd cut through the fence into which the tree had grown.

I'm sorry I wasn't there, I said, and my heart felt like it was in my feet. I kept saying how sorry I was, but it was too late. It didn't matter how softly I spoke, she couldn't hear me.

*

People look after the soil, they talk to the plants, and the gardens here are proof that people have some decency after all. I watch the gardener as he crouches down, folding himself over his own knees almost, as if he can't get his face close enough to the frozen ground.

You look worried as you lie there in your pram. I'd forgotten how worried a baby can sometimes look; you've already a wrinkle between your eyebrows, handed down from me. And you've every reason to be worried, now that you're a human being on this earth.

We pass some nursery-school children in a long line, a luminous snake of yellow vests. When one of the boys trips and falls, the grown-up holding his hand turns to the girl behind and says, Don't push Jonathan like that! But she didn't – I saw what happened and Jonathan fell over himself without any help, his legs were so short and his shoes so big. Before I can say anything, the grown-up has crouched down, gripping the girl's arm, repeating in a stern voice, No more pushing! As if it were part of the girl's nature to push. The girl, crestfallen, at a complete loss, without the language to explain that she didn't push Jonathan at all. I can hardly contain myself when I think that such things will happen to you and your brother too. He just fell, I say out loud as we walk on, he wasn't pushed at all.

I think of all the useless grown-ups we have to contend with as children, not knowing they're useless. Not until I was grown up myself did I realise that the handball trainer I'd had when I was six years old was a witch. I heard her say to the two best girls on the team that some of us didn't deserve the holdalls and T-shirts we'd been given by the postal service. I think she wanted us to hear, and after that it was never the same wearing that T-shirt, putting my kit in that hold-all, because I'd been made to think I didn't deserve it, that I wasn't good enough. Happily I stopped play-ing handball altogether and started going to football instead. It was one of the best decisions I ever made.

Your dad was so pleased when he discovered that the little red stones on the gravel pitch resembled diamonds, because then he could be with the other children after all, and while they played football he could sit by the side of the pitch and hunt for diamonds.

Being human is no easier when you're grown up, or when you're old. I can't help imagining you in a nursing home, at the end of your life. You get scared because you don't know where you are, and you can't find your money to pay for the waffels you've just eaten. You start to cry, and I'm not there to comfort you because I've been dead for ages. I can't tell you that the waffels are free and that you don't have to worry.

I imagine the heartbreaks and joys you and your brother will live through, the streets and oceans you'll cross. It's all so overwhelming.

*

It's starting to snow, the flakes melt as they touch the ground. Walking along and talking into the voice memo app on my phone, I think about my friend saying it looks like everyone's got toothache, the way they go about clasping their phones to their cheeks.

I see him in my mind's eye, standing in the classroom waving his arms about, explaining something in that enthusiastic way of his, and it seems quite inconceivable that he could die, he was so very much alive, for want of a better word. But I see him as dead too, slumped in his suit with his hair combed back, or following me around the cemetery on the outskirts of

Paris. I was searching for the grave of his favourite author for ages, and my dead friend was at my side, laughing at how useless I was. I buried him there, read some words I'd written for him, placed roses on the grave and said goodbye, and yet he kept moving about, under the headstones.

I still hear his laughter. I never knew anyone who could laugh the way he did. He sits in the Indian restaurant where we sometimes used to eat and has to pick up his napkin to dab away the tears that are rolling down his cheeks, his big, soft cheeks that always reminded me of a dog. I never knew anyone who could be as sad as him either. He's laughing at something I just said. I didn't even know I could be funny until I met him, although he didn't actually think I was funny at all. It was just that I got to him in a certain way, sparking the yes and no parts of his brain at the same time, and when that happens all you can do is laugh. To go out with someone new would be to remove his gaze from me, to replace it with another. I'd never thought of it until just now. Was that why I didn't want to go out with anyone else?

*

This isn't the sort of story to tell your child, but it's impossible to understand Bo's and my history without involving my dead friend, because why else would it take five years for us to get together? People aren't blank pages when they meet, with no past; that's not what being a human's like. Perhaps my dad thought about an old flame of his as he sat at Mum's loom, weaving tapestries, waiting for her to get ready to go out, crossing his fingers that he'd learned his lesson and that everything was going to work out better this time. It didn't, but fortunately it took thirty years for him to realise, which meant I could be born first and reach that very age, thirty.

*

He was my writing teacher. I came from my sick bed to the writing course where he taught; he was the writer who saw the writer in me, the impossible dream I nurtured of writing a novel, he saw that novel when I couldn't see it myself.

I'd never heard of him before. I sat in the first lesson listening to him; the other students said he was going to be the high point, and all I could think was, If you say so – it was what Edel used to say when we danced around the Christmas tree singing, 'To us now a saviour is born'. In the break I went off on my own, I wanted to sit in my room. But I was drawn to the classroom again and crept back in almost against my will. This is laboriously funny, he said, and indicated a passage in my work. I was horrified, and he laughed at how horrified I was. I liked him then. I realised he was a good reader, that here was the person I needed if I was going to write my book. I realised that our brains were a match.

*

When the year was over I started at another writers' school, on the other side of the country. My friend wasn't happy about it; he wanted me to start at a different school altogether, where he was going to be teaching. But I wanted to decide for myself. He'd become close – we'd be standing in the street in the middle of the night and I'd feel his breath against my neck, and it was too close, even if he took care not to be close in that sort of way. He wanted to be decent. Besides, emotionally close was far more dangerous, and in that respect he wasn't very good at protecting himself, or protecting us. It's too close! I told him. And he agreed. After I moved away, he started sending me messages at night, phoning me at night. Nearly always when I talked to him, I was in the state between being asleep and awake, and maybe that was why all the words got stuck – they churned about in my head for years. I remembered all the sentences that were uttered. I remembered all the commas and exclamation marks. Perhaps everything was stored in a special compartment of my memory, for while I seldom can remember dreams, I did remember what came in their place.

We talked about writing. I told him about the day before, when I'd got on the train and a sentence had come to me that I thought I could use, and I laughed for a long time. Yes, he replied, with warmth in his voice, and it occurred to me that I was someone a person could care about. To be perceived in that way, the way he perceived me, made all the more impression on me, I'm sure, because I'd come to the writers' school straight from being ill, from a very dark place where no one saw me at all. But still, there were some things I didn't care for – for instance, I didn't like him telling his friends about me. *I've been lauding you to the skies*, he wrote in a text, and then, *Give it to us strange.* As if I was expected to write something strange and fantastic on command that he could show to his friends; I felt like a monkey in a cage.

Then there were all the compliments, the declarations of love – you're so attractive, you're so beautiful when you laugh, and you laugh so often – words that take a person in. It's impossible not to be taken in by such words, and I wanted to be as well, but what I didn't think about was how hard it was going to be to free myself from them again. I wanted to know what we were without the words, because after a while I was no longer flattered by them; after a while I found that being sent such words made me furious. The words were a hand that closed around my heart, and I wanted my heart to beat freely and wildly. I wanted us to be friends without those strong words that displaced everything, especially because he was often drunk when he wrote them. It was a parallel dimension I no longer wanted, I started to hate it, it was a place where nothing could be relied on, where even words weren't to be relied on.

*

I've lost track of where we've been now, but the botanical gardens are on a slope, so if you lose track of where you're going you'll tend to end up at the bottom, especially if the ground is slippery and you're pushing a pram. It's like rolling down into a hollow. We're in the dark bit now, firs and pines, the Norwegian forests, their needles pricking holes in winter's thin air. You scream like an angry old woman if I do something wrong, like stop bouncing the pram, so we can't linger in this forest. We must trudge back up the hill again.

*

I finished at writers' school and debuted – my novel and I came out into the world, and for the first time I was sort of an equal to my friend. The book looked after itself, as I looked after myself, and as we started seeing each other more often I realised how badly my friend was doing. I became concerned by the way he was living, and was so upset when I got hurt, when he couldn't remember things that had happened. Yet it couldn't have been lovelier when it was just the two of us, when we went out for dinner at a restaurant, when we talked about the books we'd been reading. Everything seemed to get nicer and worse at the same time, and I didn't want to let him into my sleep any more. The power he held over me at night was too great, even if I'm not sure power is the right word. Every time he crept inside my sleep I thought of how ill he was, ill from alcohol and anxiety; he was the flame of an oil lamp, begging me to blow on him and make him flare up, longing for life and yet longing for death too, wanting to be extinguished for good. They made me so sad, those conversations we had; didn't he realise how afraid he was making me, carrying on the way he did? I couldn't bear to see him with even a beer; it made my skin creep. Every time he drank I thought of how he was killing himself by the glass. I tried to turn away from him, towards other people, but he took up so much room inside me. I care about you, he said, I've become too fond of you. And of course I was far too fond of him as well.

*

I look at you sleeping in your pram, and I know that my friend would have been glad about this, glad that I've got my own family now, glad to see me have childeren of my own. Bo and I told each other about the ghosts in our lives when we first got together. I told him about my friend, but not that much. After a while the stories we told each other changed. All of a sudden we'd be missing someone out, omitting a sentence, the stories altering a little every time they were told. The ghosts wouldn't be in them any more. I'd skip over my friend, fail to mention him, drawing breath instead, to protect myself, to protect Bo and spare us both. The question is: do ghosts get more or less dangerous when you toss a sheet over them?

*

I told my friend I wasn't going to drink any more when we were together. I felt it was wrong to drink with someone who was killing himself with alcohol, but now I'm not so sure. This was before he tried to stop – he hadn't come that far yet. I said I didn't want him to drink either. I wrote him a letter telling him how much he meant to me, how scared I was that he was going to die.

I knew I had to get away. He meant so much to me that wouldn't I die too if I stayed? There was no one incident that made me think like this, such as him still drinking regardless when we met; instead it was the sum of all incidents. We can't see each other any more, I wrote to him eventually. He probably didn't think I meant it seriously, because he still wrote to me afterwards, sent me his new book. Why could I no longer hold his hand? Why couldn't I help him up? Why didn't I think I was strong enough? I thought about these questions for years afterwards, and I still wonder if the guilt I feel means that I'm guilty.

*

We leave the forest trees and come up into the fells
– the rock garden with its frost-covered mosses. We
hear the sound of the trees as they murmur and
stretch. Soon you'll discover the real fells. You'll see
everything I can see. If the heather is lilac to you, I
won't make it crimson; the heather will only be as
splendid as it is to me if I don't describe it to you.
But then how will you learn to speak? And will you
see how splendid the heather is if I don't point it out
to you?

Everyone says to sleep when the child sleeps, but not
everyone can. I lay in the dark last night and looked
at the criss-cross of the window frames behind the
transparent curtains. I wondered which was hardest,
not sleeping or not writing. My body didn't want the
mattress, wouldn't sink down into it. I tried by turn
to will my toes, my calves, my thighs, my tummy,
into settling, but they just kept floating, and when I
tried to force them down, it was like trying to keep a
beachball below water; legs and arms and everything
else just kept popping up again. My thoughts were

stuck inside my skull, little birds fluttering about in there, like the ones in the fish heads on the Lofoten islands. Impossible to capture, they fluttered about all day, why couldn't they rest a bit at night? I tried to focus them on a book I was reading, focus my thoughts on the sentences on the page. I got up and went to the fridge, to drown the birds in milk, but it was all to no avail.

The nice thing about having children is that there's someone else besides myself to watch over at night. So instead of trying to sleep, I looked at you, while you stared at non-existent stars. *Our life is a journey, through winter and night, we look for our way, in a sky without light.*

You flapped your arms about so much, as if you were conducting our lives. We talked in your language, your sounds settled in me like warm pebbles on a beach. You were heavy in my arms, in my life, though you hardly weigh anything at all, and the badness floated off, flew away; the night passed, while you remained.

81

At some point Bo woke up too. Wait a minute, he said, then came back from the kitchen with a small glass. He put his hand behind my head, put the glass to my mouth and poured whisky inside me; that warm feeling as it ran down my throat. I asked if he could hold my foot, because I'd read in a novel how a mother held her child's foot when it couldn't sleep, but he said he wouldn't, or couldn't, and anyway it didn't matter: I slept.

*

After I broke with my friend I avoided people who knew him; I didn't have the courage to speak to anyone who might tell me something about him, just as I shied away from reading about him in the newspapers, because maybe I'd see something that told me he was already dead. Everywhere I looked I saw signs that he was going to die.

I thought I had to save him, even though we weren't in touch any more. I thought I had to write a novel so that he could understand, understand that everything could have been different. Nobody understood literature like he did; he took it to heart. I thought that if I could write a brilliant novel, about a person who changed, a novel he would realise very clearly was about him, then he would understand. When I told my publisher this, he said I'd gone mad.

My friend never got to read the novel I wrote. It wouldn't have made any difference, though at the time I believed it might. There must be something wrong with me to think I can make people want to live. The book was finished, I was just about to send him the manuscript, to phone him for the first time in two years, when I learned that he'd killed himself. I was standing on a balcony when I got the call that said he was dead, and it's as if I'm still standing there now, screaming.

It's getting harder to remember his eyes, his voice. The conversations we had recede further and further into the past and into oblivion. But the moment I found out he was dead, on that balcony, is just as vivid to me now. It will always remain in the present.

*

I'm not as angry with him now. I was so terribly angry to begin with, and for such a long time. Sometimes I do still get angry, sometimes I think he could have chosen differently, that it was all such a waste, a waste and nothing else. He was a special person, and there were people who needed him.

There are others I am still angry with, as angry as I am with myself. Every time I think about her I get angry. I was so afraid to tell her that our friend was ill because I felt I was letting him down, but she knew him, I reasoned, and so I thought I could ask her what I could do to help him. My voice was trembling. But she just laughed. She said she knew he was ill, but that he should just carry on the way he was, living hard and drinking all he could. He needs to keep on, marching towards the abyss, she said. It nearly makes me ill with bitterness to think of it.

I wish I'd managed to say something, instead of hiding from her. I hid away and left it all to her; everything I couldn't bear on my own shoulders I

84

attached to a hook that was strong enough to hold it.

*

Grief lasts such a long time, such a very long time, so long it feels like it will inhabit me for good. I didn't cry tears, I became tears; my crying consumed me and could come at any time, in the supermarket checkout while I was paying for my shopping, while trudging on my daily walks in the park. It was like being put in a room where there was nothing I decided for myself.

The grief I feel has everything it needs to thrive in my thoughts, my body, nourished there as if in a greenhouse with just the right conditions. I can't stop watering it, looking after it, as if that's what I'm here for: to love and to lose, love and lose, to love, but especially to lose. Losing my friend made me so fearful of allowing your father into my life.

*

It's half past three already and we need to collect your brother from nursery school. Your father's meeting us there. My pelvis hurts when I lift your brother up, so Bo has to be there too. But I can't help picking him up anyway; when he comes running towards me, my arms scoop him up of their own accord.

*

I've started noticing new things on our way to and from nursery school since I've been going there with your brother. We look to see if there's smoke in the chimney of the chocolate factory, if there are children sledging down the hill from the church, and we say hello to the dogs that go past: Hello, dog. Hello, dog. When men go past, your brother says, All right, mate? and if a nice girl catches his eye he pats the seat beside him in his pushchair and says, Sit down? When Bo told me your brother was flirting, I was annoyed. He's not even two years old! I said. But he does, he flirts. He's more forward than me already.

*

My biggest fear now is that I'll die and leave you behind, you and your brother, though in fact I'm more afraid you'll die and leave me behind. My own death has come closer since I've had kids; life seems longer and shorter at the same time. Shorter because I realise now that I'm not as important as I thought I was, that I'm just a tiny part of something vast and infinite. And although I'm still very much in the game, it's the children's lives that are so full of potential now. But then life seems longer when I think about how much room it gives for everything, when I think about the endlessness of childhood, and now I'm a part of my own children's childhood, an inexhaustible well of memories.

*

I've thought a lot about what my friend must have been feeling, not just during the time we weren't in touch, but in the hours leading up to his death too. I still think about it – that he knew he was going to die, that he was going to die all on his own. Did he think about the fact that he was never going to get old, not even to fifty? I think about the person he was as a child too, as if he'd been a child standing there with the rope in his hands. As a small boy, he'd been afraid of the words *bulldozer* and *growing pains*. I know he probably didn't think about that before he died, but I still do. My doctor said comfortingly that people often feel happy once they've finally made the decision. You think they must be in a terrible state, but once they've decided they can be quite euphoric, she said.

I tried to be comforted by that, but then I saw a documentary from a war-torn country which followed a young man fighting against government forces. He hid among the ruins, he couldn't sleep – every time he tried there'd be gunshots and shells exploding. Towards the end of the film he was sitting in the back of a pick-up truck on his way into an area no one could come back from alive: a conscious suicide. He sang and laughed, and it was frightening to watch, because he wasn't happy at all, but mad. It was madness that lit up his face, madness that allowed him to go towards certain death.

Sadly it's all over now, my friend wrote in a final farewell to our mutual friend, one of his very best friends – sadly it's all over now – and these words of his are the only farewell I can rely on, because in them I see the person I knew. At the same time, this 'sadly' made me distraught, for if there was no other way, then surely there was nothing to be sorry about? If he was sad that everything was over, why didn't he choose a new beginning instead? Did this 'sadly' mean that he might have wanted to live? I think it did. I think he wanted to live, but that it was too difficult for him.

*

The nursery school isn't far from the botanical gardens, but it means crossing the road three times and I've turned into a fist-shaker. Whenever I've got to wait with the pram at a crossing and the cars won't stop, I shake my fist at them. Bo gives them the finger and sometimes he'll slap the palm of his hand down on the bonnet or roof, though I've told him not to, because there are so many lunatics out there. Once, a man slammed on the brakes and jumped out and squared up to Bo. What did you do? I asked him afterwards, because I'd made myself scarce as quickly as I could, but Bo had your brother on his shoulders. Nothing – the guy knew he was in the wrong, he said.

In fact, I hadn't made myself scarce at all; time has shown that I block everything out and become paralysed in emergencies. When my dog fell in the fjord, I just stood there. She fell off the jetty right after I'd collected her from the kennel. I realised that such a small puppy probably couldn't swim, but I couldn't do anything. All I could do was stand there and say, Jump, jump! So my brother had to jump in and save her. I was paralysed too the time I pushed the pram into a revolving door and it got stuck inside. I just stood there on the pavement and the caretaker had to come and get your brother out.

Perhaps I walk in the botanical gardens because it means I'm nearby if the nursery phones and tells me to come straight away. The same day he was starting nursery, we were sitting around the table at breakfast, Bo, your brother and I, when he began to cry. He cried so much, and I didn't know why. I lifted him out of his chair and after a while he stopped, but his body was so limp in my arms, his legs wouldn't support him when I put him down. He just lay there on the floor. I turned him over to look at his face, and that was when I realised he wasn't breathing. His lips were blue. I couldn't make him respond. All I could see were the whites of his eyes. It was a feeling I can't describe; I don't know if I can say I was scared I was about to lose him – it was more like we'd lost him already. I was sure he was going to die. I thought he'd got something stuck in his throat. I can't remember if I said as much to Bo or if the same thing just occurred to him too, but Bo snatched him up and started slapping him hard on the back, yelling, No, no, no! The despair in his voice was the most painful thing I've ever heard. The child lay lifeless in Bo's arms. We ran out onto the landing and hammered on the door of our neighbour, a doctor. She held him upside down by the legs and I phoned the emergency services. Then, a sudden wail, and he was crying.

Those seconds during which he was gone will always be eternal when I think about them. The blood that trickled from his mouth, the ambulance, the paramedics, the examination, all those things remain so concrete. And then, mercifully, they told us he was all right. Bo started to cry then. The child had bitten his tongue while eating, hence the blood, and the sudden pain he felt, the shock of that, made him pass out, as if he'd been short-circuited, but there was never any danger.

I had nightmares for a long time afterwards. I dreamt I came to the nursery school and saw the child lying face down in the sandpit; he had his snowsuit on and his face was in the sand. I turned him over in slow-motion, again and again I turned him over and saw that he was blue and not breathing, night after night I turned him over, every time knowing what I was going to see. I dreamt too that I went around with a suicide pill in my purse, which I could take if he didn't recover; I looked at his face while waiting for him to start breathing again, knowing that if he didn't I'd have to swallow the pill.

*

We stop outside the old chocolate factory where the nursery is and look out for your brother's fair, home-cut hair through the window. At the same time I see Bo, my partner, your father, making his way from the other side of the park. He comes striding along on his spindly legs, towards his family. I feel self-conscious and look down at the ground, look up at the birds in the trees; for the time it takes him to cross the park I look away. And then he's there.

Hi, I say. Hi, he says, shall we go in and find the little terror? He takes my hand and I stroke his palm gently with my thumb, as if not to wake him.

It's afternoon, almost evening. The whirlwind three hours between nursery and bedtime have gusted past, buffeting us. Now your brother's asleep, Bo's in the study working and I can write again. It's not often I can write in the evenings – there's never the time, never the energy. You're three months old, I rock you with my foot as you sit in your bouncer, and I think about Per Olov Enquist, who would put his child down on the floor under his desk to play with his woolly sock while he wrote. You're clutching a giraffe in one hand and chewing on it, gripping the side of the bouncer with the other, like a passenger in a fast car who's afraid to tip over while going round a sharp curve. I must trim your nails, you've got dirt under them, are you out digging in soil when I'm not watching you?

*

This morning when Bo went off to the school of architecture I looked at him and thought to myself that he's the only person in the whole world I could have allowed into my old flat, where there was only me and my books and the dog.

There's love in a dog, but it's not enough. There's meaning in writing, but it can get to be too much. My body knew. It was as if it was withering away, as if there was something inside my chest that was dying. I felt as if I was going to fade and vanish if I kept on working every day until I dropped, but mostly if I stayed so alone. I think you should start seeing a therapist, a friend said. And then, I think you should take up pottery.

My own thoughts were that I'd soon have to let some-one in, but I didn't know how to do it any more. I was a prime number, indivisible. I'd fallen down and hurt myself so many times I almost believed love was something that no longer applied to me, that I'd been left out, and being part of two was now no longer a possibility. Love comes easy to some, but I didn't find it easy at all.

*

Loneliness wasn't the problem. My loneliness was nothing new, it wasn't something that had suddenly struck me, it was a part of me; I carry it with me like the doctor carries his stethoscope, and it's because of my loneliness I can hear if my heart's beating. Even with a child inside me I was filled with loneliness, and after the child had come out I felt empty. Loneliness lingered like a phantom pain.

Maybe it was my aloneness that made it so hard to be two, or more than two. Maybe I was too used to being on my own. But I like being on my own! Being alone, being able to sit down and write – there isn't much I appreciate more than that. I never laugh more than when I'm on my own. When I lived on my own I laughed all the time. I wrote and talked to myself and cracked up laughing. But did it mean I had to be on my own for the rest of my life?

*

Once in a while I agreed to go out with your father. For five years he asked me out for coffee, but I'd tell him I was away. He asked me out to a concert, but I wrote back and said I needed to work. He sent me music I never listened to. Only now have I heard the mad goon from the mountains sing, *Oh why, why must the same love made me laugh make me cry*. Bo gave me the novel *My Friends*, but years went by before I read it and it turned out to be one of my very favourite books. Bo would ask if I'd like to go for a walk, but I'd tell him I'd already been for a walk that day. Nearly every time he asked if we should do something together I told him no, and nearly every time he gave up on me. Months would pass, years, in between our seeing each other.

I was standing at the bus stop, it was a day in spring. You were standing there waiting when I got off the bus, Bo said later. You looked like you'd been standing there for ever, and I thought to myself then that maybe it was important to you after all that we met. We walked through narrow streets with old houses

97

on each side, and I could have lived there, or there, and he could too. Out of the blue Bo said it drove him mad to see small children – he so much wanted children of his own! I looked at him, unable to understand that he could say something like that out loud. I'd never been able to admit to anyone that I wanted children, because what if I never had any? Then they'd have to live with the disappointment as well.

I had to stop as I walked along next to Bo, because I suddenly thought about my family sitting at the kitchen table, the family I grew up in. We sat at the creaky table with the oilcloth on it, one brother to my right on the bench, the microwave on its shelf to my left. I hated sitting by the microwave, it blew air straight into my ear, air I was convinced must be radioactive. Dad sat at the end, my other brother on the adjustable chair opposite me, and Mum by the window. We shared a tin of meatballs. I've no idea how we survived – we hardly ate. I loved my family, and I pictured myself then having to sit on my own at the kitchen table for the rest of my life. The prospect of that, which all of a sudden felt like a probability: that I wasn't ever going to have a family of my own.

I couldn't bear it. It couldn't happen. We'll have kids, then, I said. We'll help them on and off with their little boots every day, push the heavy pram all the way home from nursery in the dark with the shopping bag full of milk and fish-fingers dangling at the side. Yes, said Bo. But it didn't occur to me we'd be doing it together.

*

I know the story of how my mum and dad found each other off by heart. I've always been fond of it, untainted as it is by sorrow or hardship or ghosts of the past, though I'm sure there's a lot I don't know about. Dad was out on the town with his mates and one of them had taken some others along, among them my mum. She warned him not to drink more than a pint, and, blushing, told him about the time she'd drunk two and couldn't remember a thing the next day. That was when they started going out, just the two of them on their own. My dad likes to be in plenty of time, whereas my mum's pretty much always last minute, so while he was waiting for her to get ready one night, he tried his hand at weaving on the big loom they had in the living room at my mum's house. He ended up weaving several tapestries in the time they were courting. And then at last my mum would be standing there beside him in an ironed skirt and her hair washed, though more likely she'd have preferred to be in her work blouse. The best bit is when Mum tells us what Dad eventually said to her one day: You're the one I want.

The story I'm telling you about your father and me ought really to be as simple as that. There, in mid-tapestry, I turn towards Bo and say: You're the one I want.

*

When Bo and I went for that walk and imagined ourselves moving into all the houses we saw, he mentioned in passing the holiday plans he and his partner had for the summer. So the thought of the two of us being a couple must have occurred to me, because why else would this feel like a slap in the face? I didn't know he had a partner, and felt he should have told me a lot earlier.

You're a demon, I said, a *demon*. It's hard for me to understand now my choice of that exact word, *demon*, but at the time it felt appropriate. I'd recently been to a play about demons, so that probably had something to do with it. I said the word several times, staring fixedly ahead as we walked up a never-ending hill, but I still only thought of him as a friend, so what right did I have to be disappointed? I said the word *demon* so many times that eventually he became annoyed.

Yet he couldn't bring himself to say goodbye, to part, as we stood at the bus stop that evening. It feels wrong not knowing where you live, he said. I pointed over at my building. My flat's the one that looks like it's on fire, I said. From the street it did look like it was on fire – it was the orange lampshade in the living room.

*

I hope you can see the romance in this. That I took him from someone else. That he left his partner for me. You can see the malice in it, but there's romance too.

Bo remembers romance in that walk too. I fished his sunglasses out of the river with a stick after he lost them playing with the dog. He told me how happy it made him, and I was surprised that such a small and trivial thing can bring two people together. I hardly gave it a thought at the time. Mostly I was surprised that I could be romantic.

You set the alarm on a Saturday? he exclaimed the first weekend he spent the night at my place. I'd set the alarm for six-thirty so I could get up and work – it was what I always did. I scrabbled over him and hopped onto the floor before realising how gob-smacked he was.

It was still a while before we were properly a couple, but something happened that day we walked together: the realities hit me on the head like a brick. Bo was in a relationship, he had someone. People were enjoying real relationships while I just sat at home on my own, writing about relationships that had gone wrong.

Then Bo moved to Paris, and something important must have happened on our walk, because I missed him. I wasn't prepared for that.

*

The child fell asleep almost before I'd sung for him, he was so tired. Whenever he's worn out like that he gets scared by fluff on the floor, the light on the vacuum cleaner, by shadows on the wall, and fruit flies. I brushed his teeth, quietly counting to ten as he sat in the bathroom doorway – he likes to sit on the threshold – and when we'd finished he clapped his hands and cried, Bravo, bravo!

I lay down next to him in the bed and smoothed his hair with my hand. You're the best little boy in all the world, I said, and then he said, Over! So I turned over and lay with my back to him, and he said, Gakk-gakk

– goodnight – before giving me a peck on the back of my head and letting out a sigh: Ahhh. Every time he kisses us, we say, Ahhh, because we think he's so good – that must be why he's started saying it himself.

*

The first time I saw Bo was in a mirror. He was a friend of a friend and I was standing in front of the mirror in the loo of a bar where the launch party for my first book was being held. It must have been a kind of unisex toilet, and he must have noticed me talking to myself – I was so nervous about speaking to people about my novel for the very first time – and he said into the reflection that there was no need to be nervous. He said the job was already done, the book would be the same no matter what, nothing I said could ruin it now.

We celebrated in the warm night. I was bewildered to be throwing a party, with coloured lights and happy people, and I was overwhelmed by everyone who had come and who I cared about, yet I still felt dreadfully despondent. I didn't understand a thing about the world – I couldn't make sense of things. You're standing in a puddle, a friend said. I was standing in a puddle in my prettiest dress, but I hadn't noticed. All I was aware of was how unhappy I was. I was unhappy even though the novel was finished, unhappy that my friend was falling apart – he was the one who'd helped me see what the book could become. He stood in the midst of the party with one foot at the abyss. I was already grieving for him , but I had no idea then how great it would become. He pushed me away, I withdrew, and was attracted by Bo, this unfamiliar, good-looking man; he looked kind too. I was surprised I could be interested in any-one else but my friend, and I realise as I'm writing this now that that was when it happened – the shift from my friend to Bo. That was the turning point. Perhaps I shaped the story about Bo and me, the two of us together, right from that very first encounter, without realising it myself.

His body radiated something – something that meant his body pulled me towards it, that single body in a sea of people, and we almost kissed. I felt it in my stomach. We stood so close, as close as you can without being too close. You can't stand that close to someone without thinking about kissing them. I nearly kissed someone I didn't know – it had never happened to me before. The way he looked at me, I still remember that.

Bo asked if we could write to each other. I didn't know what he meant. Write? I imagined finding letters dropped into my letter box, how serious that would be, and I didn't have the courage to meet him in writing. Writing weighed so heavily inside me, writing had become something big and scary to me, which could change everything.

Besides, my dying friend still took up so much room. He was standing further away, with a cigarette in one hand, gesticulating with the other. People stood in a ring around him. How could I save him, how could I leave him? Don't leave me, he said, don't forgive me, he said.

*

Years after I'd stood in that puddle, I realised I'd written a novel about a dog that turned out to be a child. It strikes me as ironic now that it was perhaps the writing that prevented me from starting a family. Its spell was too strong in a way; the power of my imagination was stronger than my ability to see the world as it was. Writing became an excuse for living a loveless life. The child was a melody that hadn't been played. To become someone's partner is the most complicated and the most banal thing a person can do, the thought of it almost made me poorly. I wouldn't be able to be with someone who was wrong for me. I get ill so quickly when I make a bad decision – the illness comes back then and suffocates me.

Besides, I didn't know how to look after another person; life was hard enough as it was. After I was ill, when I could still hardly look after myself, I couldn't possibly see myself being useful to others. So I got myself a plant, a peace lily, to prove to myself I could have a dog; and then I got a golden retriever to prove to myself I could have a partner and a child. The peace lily bit isn't entirely true, but nearly, because I did actually worry when it looked limp and wonder if

I could even keep a plant alive. The golden retriever bit is true. Could I be as hard on myself as I am and at the same time devote time and care to a living creature?

*

I wondered why it got to me so much that Bo had a partner. So I wrote to him in Paris, asking him if he could read the novel I was working on, about this lonely thirty-three-year-old woman and her dog (or was it a child?), because I thought maybe then I could find out what was going on.

Before long, summer had come and Bo was briefly back in Oslo. He brought my unfinished manuscript with him, with all his thoughts and comments. He was going to give me his reading of it, which is the finest gift a person can give. But first he wanted to show me something.

Bo told me the city had built a studio for Gustav Vigeland in exchange for the donation of his entire body of work up until that time, as well as what he would produce in the future, a studio that would later be turned into an art museum. I couldn't grasp how Vigeland had the courage to agree, to give away everything that was his, including his less successful works; it sounded like such a risk. But if the right circumstances are provided, which make a person feel secure, perhaps the heart will be free to beat wildly and without restraint, perhaps they then find the courage to give their heart away?

Bo and I were the only ones in the big museum – apart from the woman at the desk, who looked after my dog – and it felt as if Bo and I were on our own in the world. I looked at Vigeland's unfinished works and it struck me that these were perhaps the ones I liked the best, more than looking at the finished monolith – I liked the feeling of being allowed an insight into something secret, something off-kilter, whose mistakes and shortcomings remained visible. Maybe it didn't matter if my manuscript was a bit of a failure, that I too was a bit of a failure?

In the middle of the building was an open courtyard with some benches, the only logical place to sit and talk. We skirted it for an age, as if unable to get to the heart, to talk about what we were meant to talk about. I thought about whether this was what we'd been doing for five years, and I wondered how long I could keep an innocent face.

Eventually, Bo suggested we go and sit down, and my legs followed his out into the open, beneath the tall sky. Four walls of red brick surrounded the courtyard and it was as if the museum had turned to face us and was looking at us, instead of the other way round. I was filled by a strange sense of calm. Yes, I said, though he hadn't asked me anything.

*

It grieves me that we didn't realise sooner that we belonged together, Bo said last night, though it could just as easily have been another night. He says this often. I stroked my finger over his forehead, like an eraser, or an apology. The first time he said it, my immediate reaction was no, not at all, everything's for the best! But then I realised he was right. I threw away our past. What could have been our past belongs now to some other couple. We could have had lots more children, as Bo says, even though he might not have wanted that many. But I might have. Now I'll soon be too old to have lots of children. I came late to literature, I discovered love late, I've had children late.

*

Bo went back to Paris and gradually, gradually I started to understand a thing or two. Realising you need to make changes to your life is so agonising and so frightening. Some years back I'd got myself too involved in what was only *nearly* something. I'd taken part in a literature festival and fallen for a married man in a foreign country, and I comforted myself with the thought that this love would still give me time to write. I still thought then that the safest thing was to only write about love. But then, nothing ever happens if all you want is to be safe.

111

This won't work out with you being married, I told him over the phone, though I'm always afraid of hurting people. My honesty ruined it for him – the game he was playing, the pretend world he was setting up. By being honest I stopped him from living in his fantasy, and stopped myself from living in mine too. He was stunned. I can't believe this is happening now, he said, before anything's even happened! It's like everything's fast-forwarding, this isn't supposed to happen for another two years! Two years, he said. It was my turn to be stunned then. That he could think like that, as if he'd been planning for it to end, but only after keeping hold of me for two years! I didn't deserve that.

I won't tell you any more about him, or about any of the others either, for there have been others, but I turn them into one, the people I've loved, or thought I could love. They come together, all my previous infatuations merge into one, the way the branches of a tree join at the trunk, which is rooted in the ground. I bury them there. It's up to me what kind of image I keep, it's up to me alone.

*

Mostly it's about having the courage to make a decision. With your head as well as your heart. And there was a name that kept cropping up in my head and in my heart, time and again, like a prayer, all through the days, the weeks that followed. I thought about Bo as I walked with my dog in the park, and one night I understood something important: I never saw my loneliness so clearly as when I was with him. There were others I could entertain, perhaps even impress a bit, but I couldn't do that with Bo – he never made me feel I was better, funnier or cleverer than I am. This might sound sad, but in my writing I'm no better than the person I actually am. At the same time, my loneliness became less of a threat, because with Bo I understood that, with him, I was good enough, the same way that I'm good enough in my writing.

When I got home that night I opened the door of the flat with caution, afraid that the words on the cupboard door in the kitchen might have been erased, that someone had wiped away the words like chalk from a blackboard. *I wake up at night, I see the other side*

113

of the world / still, that's not the way I'll reach you. I'd been staring at these words that Bo had sent me, which I'd written on the cupboard door with a permanent marker. I'd read them over and over, but I hadn't written anything in reply. The words were still there when I came in, and it occurred to me then what they meant: *I wake up in the world and the night, see the other side of me, and that's the way I'll reach you.* I'd only ever seen myself, and now I had to see the other side of this 'myself' to see Bo.

I snatched up my phone, as if I'd just made some life-changing decision, only to be assailed by compulsive thoughts about saying something that could ruin everything. But maybe it was the same with us as it was with the book – what he said to me in the mirror the first time we met: the important part was already done and I wouldn't be able to ruin what was between us even if I said something stupid or wrote the wrong thing. Maybe our single words didn't have to weigh a ton and cause the world to turn back on itself.

*

It was a good idea – clever, wise almost – to phone your father that night. If you ever wonder about whether to phone someone or not, I'd say, go on, do it. You've got to talk to people in order to get on, it's no good just thinking about them, writing about them, sometimes you've got to make yourself heard. They might be accommodating, or you might fall flat on your face and hurt yourself, but you've got to take the chance if you want to find out who they are.

*

Bo told me on the phone about his fear of getting ill, going mad, that he wanted peace. I realised he was broken. He'd said the same things to me before, but I hadn't taken him seriously then. He was only thirty, but he was used up, worn out, finished. I thought about the time we walked by the river, before I understood that we were going to be a couple, although I'd started to realise where it was heading. It was something to do with his jumper. I'd noticed his grey cotton jumper when he got off the bus and gave me a hug; he was so clean and nice and warm

115

and smelled so good – he'd only just showered after going for a run, and it was as if the trees and the sky and everything he'd seen while he was out running had been absorbed by his skin, I wanted to keep smelling him.

After our walk, we went into a pub around the corner from where I lived. They had cheap red wine and plastic flowers on the tables and dark wooden walls that weren't wood at all. I thought Bo seemed down, especially when he was talking about something that interested him – it was as if it was all in the past. You talk as if life's been and gone, I said. I can't understand how I could bring myself to say such a thing. He seemed to unravel in front of me, his eyes grew moist, as if he'd been waiting for someone to say this to him, to see how lost he was. At that moment I saw him more clearly than I'd done before, but it was still a picture with too much backlight.

He told me how sad it made him to see me, because it was only with me he felt he was alive. It was rather too much for me to take in, and I acted like it was nothing.

116

You bought your shares while they were at an all-time low, Bo says, referring to himself. He hit rock bottom the summer before we got together, when he was living in France and the only thing he could think of to keep himself sane was measuring windows. While we spoke on the phone that night I pictured him walking about Paris. As soon as the day started he went out into the streets with his tape measure in his pocket. He took the metro in the mornings, to the end of the line with the other workers. As they went off to their offices, he set off back home on foot. He wore a peaked cap so the houses and lamp posts didn't intrude on his field of vision. People were too much, the ground in front of him was more than enough.

He had legs and feet like a little bird; a gust of wind could have blown him over at any minute. His legs moved as if he were climbing a steep flight of stairs – he bent his knees and lifted his feet high, using all his energy, almost planting his feet into the ground again, down into the pavement, with every step he took. If he was attached to the sky, the string must

117

have been very thin, it was as if it could snap whenever. But in his hand he held the tape measure. He measured doors, measured windows, and he wrote down the name of the street and the measurements. In that way he knew he existed, even if he existed outside of time.

*

You know a person for five years, and then all at once you see that person in a completely different way. I'd known everything about him, but he was a stranger then; only now did I begin to understand. I asked him about the quote from Hamsun's *Pan*: *I love three things, I go on. I love a dream of love I once had, I love you, and I love this spot of ground. And which do you love most? The dream.*

Which do you love most? I asked Bo, and to my disappointment he replied that, like me, he loved the dream of love most. The loss we would experience in either case was the same. Reality was no better than that.

He worked with plasterboard, exhibiting in galleries, but most of all, and this was what he preferred, he loved to sit in his studio and stare at what he was working on. He gave so little away about it that he basically excluded most people from grasping what it was about. I wondered if his work was like being in love with someone from a distance – whether he was keeping it to himself because he knew that every time he revealed something about it to someone he'd be disappointed by their reaction, and the more often it happened, the more hopeless it all would become.

*

As suddenly as the leaves began to fall from the trees, your father came home from Paris. I'll tell you about that autumn later in more detail; thinking about it makes me feel so strange in my mind, perhaps because everything seemed mostly to be about plasterboard, so I'll tell you about the winter instead.

Bo was standing outside the door with his little backpack and was dreadfully thin. He'd left his partner

119

and was only going to be staying at mine while I was away, at least that's what I pretended, because deep down I was wondering if he couldn't just stay for good. I thought it was time to live in the fast lane a bit, to challenge my inertia, but I didn't let on to Bo. I'd cleared one of the bookshelves from top to bottom to make him feel welcome. He put his toothbrush there, and we stood and looked at the empty bookshelf with his toothbrush on it.

While I was away I thought about him being there in the flat. I pictured him moving around amongst my things, passing a finger over the spines of the books, resting his head on my pillow, getting to know me even if I wasn't there.

When I got back I stood for a while on the pavement looking up at the kitchen window. I was so used to coming home to a dark and empty flat, but now it looked as if there was a fire burning inside. A person was standing in my kitchen, a person who was waiting for me, who'd made pizza for when I came home. I was reminded of my family.

*

It was a cold winter and I tried to stop myself feeling down because Bo was not oozing happiness. He lay on the sofa with his hoodie pulled over his face, having to start from scratch again. It was the limit of what he could manage. It was so depressing with that hoodie; how would we cope in the long run if things were depressing now? He wandered about on his spindly legs, looked in the fridge, which looked emptily back, and I hoped he was on his way out of his darkness. I saw the darkness seeping out of him, leaving a black mark on the floor.

We had to wear so much clothing during the day, and shivered naked together under the covers at night. Bo ran a fever and turned to the wall. He hadn't any strength left; I could have hung him up on a peg next to my coat. We fell ill, both of us. There was too much resistance, too much will inside us, we were like two wild horses tied together. It was as if we had to be ill in order to succumb, to give ourselves up and surrender completely.

The bed was like a hammock, we rolled together in the middle, like two bits of gravel in a length of guttering. We clung to each other, shoved each other away. There was no escape. The soft mattress determined that we belonged together.

I felt for his hands under the cover, my back felt for his back, my tummy snuggled up to his tummy, our bodies wanting to be close. I used to be so alone before, when there was no one to share with. Now we were two, sharing our innermost feelings in the middle of the bed. But there was no protection there.

We filled the nights with words – we knew so little about each other's lives. I didn't know he hadn't gone to nursery school until he was six. He had to lock himself in the loo to be able to think, and the loo was too small for that, his thoughts couldn't fit. Since then he hasn't been able to fit anywhere, which makes him like himself less, while I like him that much better. I also like the story about when he had to write a letter to his grandfather. It was going all right for a while, but then he realised there wasn't enough room on one line to finish the letter, that the last words would have to go on the next line, and so he decided not to write to his grandfather after all, and threw the pencil at the wall.

We couldn't sleep. The thought of it made us feel we'd be leaving each other. I wanted to know everything about him – about his hands when they'd still belonged to a child, folded, his fingers interlaced. They had to be touching; if they weren't there'd be no connection and no one would be able to hear him. We couldn't lose each other now. Sleeplessness lay throbbing under our skin, right until morning.

*

I got better before him. He was still wrapped in fever, like a damp sweater. His teeth chattered, he snuggled up to me for warmth, telling me how cold he felt, but he was burning hot, it was like lying next to a stove.

Bo was worried because we both needed this, the two of us together, we needed it so badly. I didn't want him to be worried, I wondered if he was saying we were no good after all. He said hurtful words, words about himself that no one else would have said, but he couldn't talk to me about it, because I kept hearing 'we' whenever he said 'I'. I always think everything's about me. He said other things too that were even more hurtful, not because what he said was completely untrue, but because he was right in a way.

I thought he was going to disappear, that he couldn't be with me when he felt so bad about himself; I thought I was going to lose myself. I wanted to get away. I was so afraid of getting close to people who came apart. I hadn't the strength for that any more; I was too close to the abyss as it was.

To make us feel better, I told him about the time I served him cinnamon rolls, even though he was there himself and could hardly have forgotten. I told him about how I'd taken the frozen rolls out of the freezer and arranged them on a dish in front of him, how nice everything had looked, and how appalled Bo had been. And then you realised how funny it was, I said. I couldn't stop laughing, tossing my head back and holding my stomach, and Bo laughed with me. Only I laughed for so long that after a while he didn't know what to do with himself, he seemed at a loss, and I apologised because he'd stopped laughing ages ago. I gave him a nod as if to confirm that it was he who was in the right. Once I start laughing, I said, laughing again, people find me embarrassing. And then I manage to stop.

We turned away from each other, we hurt each other. It felt like having a great big comb dragged through me, all the teeth ripping me apart on the inside, making my body tremble. He was so weary from not feeling any firm ground underfoot, and I was so scared of loving him, I kept dying of fright the whole time. I struck him in the heart, said something that made him turn away, or maybe it was just me turning away that made him do the same. But then I couldn't sleep with him at such a distance.

Eventually it was something else that germinated in me, something else that came over me. One night, I'd come back from a Christmas get-together with friends. Bo hadn't wanted to go and I couldn't understand why. When I got home I found him curled up in bed, lying there like a pile of forgotten clothes. My first instinct was to turn round and go back out again, but instead I found I was able to sit down on the edge of the bed and I smoothed my hand over his hair, his lovely, troubled head. I said that this too would pass. If I looked after myself, then surely I'd manage to be there for him?

He slept through the days, slept away the fever, and then when he got well again he was changed. He looked refreshed – it was plain in his face. He looked stronger than before he'd been ill.

*

You're four months old now. You're unhappy sitting in your chair. So I put you down on the mat. You roll over onto your tummy, intentionally, and roll back again, unintentionally, looking up at me in bewilderment. I can't help but laugh, and then you laugh too, your arms and legs waving in the air, and then after a while you're too tired. You no longer know if you're laughing or crying. I lift you up and hold you in the crook of my arm, I can write with my left index finger at the keyboard while you sleep there. But you don't want to sleep, you refuse to give in to it, and when you realise there's no other way, you give out a heart-rending cry.

*

We had to move out of my flat. It was like an old slipper I'd worn for too long – it wouldn't fit anyone else but me. The four walls seemed almost to press in on our lungs, we could hardly breathe in there, and, although she was gentle, the dog was a force that could knock us for six. Bo thought my dog was too doggy for him to be able to relate to, but too human for him to ignore. I felt he'd discovered her soul, though I didn't let on. They played and sized each other up, trying to fathom each other, understanding nothing. I could forget she was even there, often becoming aware of her only when she wasn't, and then I missed her. Bo was aware of her all the time, he couldn't bear it if he thought she was bored, and would wake her up so she wouldn't be. He hid tit-bits inside towels for her to find, and rolled her up in blankets. Snoozing on the sofa that was far too small for him, he would wake with a start when she came and nudged him. One day he looked at me and said in all seriousness: This is probably a major transition for her too.

So we moved into a flat with more room, up above the trees, but we forgot to think about all that was good in the old flat, how quiet the streets were there, how easy life can be with only one room.

*

It didn't help that we managed to get all our books shelved in the new study, for the rooms kept moving; we moved the furniture from room to room, we moved ourselves from room to room, and nothing seemed to fit. I could stand there thinking I was in the middle of the living room, with space all around me, only to feel the peace lily on the windowsill tickle my arm and realise I was in a different room altogether, a smaller one. I didn't know where to eat, where I could write. Every other day I'd wake up in a new room, I'd wake up on Bo's side of the bed, on the sofa or an inflatable mattress, usually in a room full of clutter, clothes horses and paintbrushes. If nothing else, I know now that I sleep in the same place as you. When I wake up you're lying close to me. You always lie so very close to me.

For Bo it's as if other people's lives always take up more room than his own. He looks at the worn flooring in the kitchen and it's as if the previous inhabitant is still dragging their chair between the counter and the place where their dining table must have been, fetching a glass of water without getting up. Bo hears that chair dragging backwards and forwards, backwards and forwards. We'll have to sand the floor so we can leave our own marks, he says. Often he'd sit on the sofa in the evenings looking worried, and for a long time I couldn't bring myself to ask what he was thinking about – I was sure it was us. But then one day I asked him, and he said, The floor plan. Old solutions are hidden away behind new, poorer solutions. These were Bo's words; I haven't got those kinds of words for what's wrong with the flat. All I know is I miss the woods.

*

I can't get around telling you about the autumn: our first autumn together. I'd phoned your father in the middle of the night, but I remember so little of what happened after that. Something must have happened, obviously – he can't just have moved straight into the flat. I must have managed to say something, I must have said: You're the one I want.

He came back to Oslo. The wind whirled the leaves around me as I walked through the streets trying not to imagine the worst that could happen. Him deciding to stay with his partner, that it would be she who cleared the space inside him that needed to be cleared. I read in a book: *I have noticed that doing the sensible thing is only a good idea when the decision is quite small. For the life-changing things you must risk it. And here is the shock – when you risk it, when you do the right thing, when you arrive at the borders of common sense and cross into unknown*

*territory, leaving behind you all the familiar smells and lights;
then you do not experience great joy and huge energy. You are
unhappy. Things get worse. It is a time of mourning. Loss.
Fear. We bullet ourselves through with questions. And then we
feel shot and wounded.*

I dreamt his partner was sitting in a car. She couldn't
get hold of him on the phone and she looked despair-
ingly at me as I stood there in front of her in the
middle of the crossing. He's gone mad! she shouted
through the windscreen. Then she showed me the
gestures he made when he was mad, batting the air
like a person trying to catch flies in their bare hands.
Bo had a flat with an old, heavy piano in it, and a
partner he'd been together with for several years; I
couldn't fathom how they were going to get the piano
down all those stairs.

I read the label on the bottle of pills that was on the
kitchen counter: *Magnesium helps the heart relax between
beats.* So I wrote to him, managing to be a bit savvy,
to be patient for once. I wrote that I'd wait until he'd
concluded whatever he had to conclude, I'd wait
until he was ready, there was no hurry. Just a bit. He'd

been waiting five years, surely I could wait a while too. He had to get things sorted, properly. I'll wait for you, I wrote. But what if he'd already changed his mind, what if I stood waiting outside a door that was closed?

*

.

That horrible autumn, that dreadful limbo. But at the same time something very wonderful happened too. I asked Bo if he wanted to come over for pancakes. I was convinced he'd say no. But he said he'd absolutely love to come for pancakes. I'd barely ever made dinner for anyone before. We had pancakes and I was wearing a blouse I thought looked good but which I suddenly decided was quite ugly halfway through the meal, and then Bo had to go home, because there was a partner there waiting for him.

I asked if he'd like to come to a reading I was doing, from the children's book I'd written. I had to sit on something not even remotely like a chair, and only Bo and three children came. I'd never read for children before, so my hands were shaking. I hadn't the courage to look at Bo, not even once. But he said such nice things to me afterwards that left me at a loss for words. I wondered why. Why did I think I didn't deserve someone who said things like that?

I had to decide to trust him. I had to keep on deciding, over and over. Whenever I neared the perilous waters of unease and felt that I couldn't go through with it, that I hadn't got it in me to wait any longer, that it was better to put an end to it now rather than later, I forced myself to steer another course and seek out the feeling of trusting us both. Love takes time, I told myself, like a mantra. We're dealing with people. It's a process.

Then one day he said: I'd like you to see my studio. Our trajectories were different from before. We circled each other, weaved in and out and around. I was aware of his every movement, his eyes glancing then glancing away. I sat in the green corduroy chair that was normally his; it was as close to him as I dared to get. He showed me how to use his camera and I took a photo of him before we left – he was standing behind the desk putting a book into his bag. I dig that photo out now as I sit writing; it's been a while since I've looked at it. He's smiling timidly, I think he looks peaceful.

We sat next to each other on the bus home and I hardly had it in me to move. After he got off at his stop he sent me a text that said that all he wanted was to put his head on my shoulder. He's always had pluck, your dad. It made me so happy; I pictured us together, properly together.

*

Oddly, I became more scared of losing Bo after he moved in with me. I still am scared; for instance I get scared of losing him just writing these sentences, as if somehow they'll become a spell – I can be superstitious when the mood comes over me. As scared as I've been of your father dying, I've been more scared of losing him to someone else. It's my own fault. Maybe I was scared because I'd stolen him? I may have given the impression that your father was the only broken one of us two, but that's not the way it was.

I thought love meant discovering a new person, but it's more discovering yourself, and that's painful. Who would have thought I could be jealous? It was a side of me I'd never known before. Or if I did, I'd suppressed it.

*

I hardly knew who your father and I were together when we were on our own, so I definitely didn't know who we were when we were with others. Still, we went to a party together – this time Bo wanted to go. We made ourselves vulnerable, putting ourselves in front of other people, the couple we now were, vulnerable to something we didn't know. How far could we go before our hope-filled blue sky turned into a dismal darkness?

People were hanging out of the windows, sitting on the floor in clouds of cigarette smoke. Bo's ex was there. The past is always there somewhere at parties – a soggy newspaper in someone's raincoat pocket. I pretended not to care, and wasn't the reason I found her so threatening that she struck a tender spot in me? This was surely more about me than her, so where did this uncertainty come from?

I stood chatting to an actor with no soul. I'd read about this in a book, about how there were people without a spirit or soul, and now I felt I'd met one. I couldn't concentrate on what he was saying, because Bo was nowhere to be seen. I couldn't form sentences, never mind conduct a conversation if Bo was gone. I tried to organise my thoughts as they might have been written down in my diary, so that I might understand and find him again somewhere between the lines, but the only words I found were: *goodbye, perhaps*. Eventually I left the actor to go and look for him. I went from room to room, each a hum of loud voices, half-empty bottles everywhere, but just as I was about to go out onto the balcony and see if he was there, I stopped myself and turned back, as if knowing what I would find out there.

Bo and I walked home in the snow together, our heavy boots sinking in at every step. This sorrow, all that had to be resolved. What was to become of us? I said nothing but remained as quiet as before. I didn't tell him I hadn't been able to find him, I left that unsaid. But it was the only thing I could think about: *I couldn't find you.*

Although he was no longer running a fever, I burnt myself when I touched him, and that night, walking under all that falling white, I wasn't sure I knew deep down if we were going to be all right.

*

You're such a bonny baby. It's a sentence that feels oddly old-fashioned on my tongue, but still I can't help saying it. A bonny baby. I see the veins at your temple, your sleeping hand as it grips my jumper, your face; you're the image of Bo.

I've always thought there was something famil-iar about your brother, from the very moment I saw him, and he's turned out to be a carbon copy of my youngest brother. In my dreams they're often the same person, like last night when I had another nightmare about finding him face down in the sand-pit. I thought I was finished with those nightmares.

*

Bo and I went to a private view at a gallery. When you're an artist you've got to do these things, put yourself about, be social in the right circles. I thought Bo and I had got better at being together – together with other people – that we were steadier now as a couple. But I didn't know how awful private views can be. It had barely begun when a black limo came and picked up a small group who'd been selected to have dinner together, while the rest of us were left behind. All we could do was go on with the party as if nothing had happened.

I studied them, the artists. Their aesthetic sense was strong; they looked different from writers. I suppose it's harder being an artist than being a writer – writers can hide themselves away more, wear untrendy trousers; writers aren't meant to belong, to fit in.

I hid myself away, glass in hand, which is to say I stood at the bottom of the big staircase where Bo was sitting, but he didn't see me, he saw someone else instead. She was pretty. The way he looked at her, the way he took a sip from her beer glass and smiled, not out of politeness, but warmly, his face lighting up, made me shrivel and wither, until I felt like a sad sprig of wild chervil in autumn. Love is such a serious matter.

I knew I had to make myself heard; I owed it to us. I couldn't give up now, or do as the Japanese do when the soul is pained: slice up my stomach.

Clinging to her, I repeated after we got home that night, my eyes running black. The words were so strong, so hurtful to speak, especially to him, especially to someone who feels they're on the outside. The moment I heard myself I realised that the reason he'd lit up was because on the stairs he'd felt like an insider, for a moment he'd no longer been on the outside. But

I heard the vulnerability in my voice too, and wondered if he was going to put his arms around me.

The jealousy left me as soon as I took that firm stand. The painful thoughts slid away like figure skaters on an ice rink. But as the jealousy left me, Bo's anger rose, all the way up to his eyes. I barely recognised his voice – it was as if he'd been dubbed by someone else. He was so angry with me that I had no idea who I was and forgot everything I knew about myself. I doubted I'd ever known anything. It was as if I didn't even know what I was called, and was unable to trust my own name.

Yet strictly speaking it wasn't the night I ruined, it was the day after. Thoughts aren't the truth, I told myself in order to breathe. I'm not my thoughts, I'm not my feelings, am I? Writing, which keeps me afloat, didn't help, because I didn't write, I just sank and sank.

I couldn't look at him as we navigated our way around each other in the flat. We were so distraught, had no idea what to do, and we thought the situation belonged to the place where it started, the place where we were, and that we had to stay there in order to make it better, but it all just got worse and worse. We realised we had to get away, and I checked to see when the next ferry was leaving for Denmark, the next plane to Dublin, and then we got on a coach to Gothenburg.

The journey was awful. I kept changing from wanting to cry on his shoulder and twine my hair into his, to planning to get off at the next stop and leave him, but I didn't want to leave him.

We both had so many cracks, we needed to repair each other. Eventually he put his hand to my cheek. Nature's ability to heal, the body's ability to heal. He said we should never lose each other like that again. We walked through the streets of Gothenburg and didn't let go of each other's hands.

*

I see now that it's not fair to write that Bo sipped from her glass. Writing that sentence felt like a punch in the stomach. No one sips from another person's glass. I can't show him up like that, even if that's what he did.

Bo? I call out. Bo? He appears in the doorway of the study, looking handsome and befuddled. Can I ask you something? Of course, he says. How's your project going? Bo's been rather preoccupied of late, which he's allowed to be; I am too, or still am. He's preoccupied because he's drawing a home for us, designing a flat in which I can sleep, write and drink coffee.

I wanted to ask you, I say, interrupting him, because I've got to ask him even though I'm dreading it. Do you remember that night we argued so terribly we had to go to Gothenburg, after we'd been to that private view together, when you took a sip from that woman's glass? Bo laughs and says he did no such thing; he couldn't have taken a sip from someone else's glass, he'd never do anything like that.

*

142

We moved in with each other before we were really together, moved into a new flat before we'd got used to being together in the old one, and we mixed our books from the start. For years I'd been covering the walls with bookshelves, filling the shelves with books, they had become so thick and safe. Now we mixed Bo's books with mine. It was a kind of obligation; his books were the most important thing he had, and the same was true for me – my books and my dog. The dog's got a name, she's called Beckett. The first word the child said was 'Beckett'. Now Bo's books had become mine, and vice versa.

I kept having to ask myself how to live with another person. Was I meant to kiss his cheek before going to the kitchen for a glass of water, was I meant to tell him when I was going to bathroom? I couldn't just go without saying anything, or could I? And what did it mean if we weren't sitting in the same room, when I was sitting in one room wondering what he was thinking in the other? Was I meant to go in and ask, just to make sure?

*

I was no longer alone at breakfast: Bo was facing me. I saw him as this quiet person, a quiet soul, but something had filled him up with noise. Even when he wasn't saying anything, when he was just sitting quietly across the table from me, I could hear the noise inside him. I didn't think anyone else could hear it, it was like dogs and dog whistles; I was the only one who could hear his shrill, piercing noise, and I recognised that noise in my own. He found no rest, and his restlessness bled from his ears, his tear ducts, seeped through his skin.

Bo didn't cry when he was born. No one knows when he cried for the first time. One day his mother was getting ready to have a shower; she put Bo down on the floor below the windowsill so he couldn't fall off anything, and instead a potted plant fell on him. His mother heard a crash and ran into the living room to see Bo lying there with the shards of the pot like a halo about his head, the cactus across his throat and his face covered in soil. He just looked at her, scrutinised her at length through all the soil.

*

One night as we were crossing the road that first winter, Bo said he sometimes wondered if I actually liked him. I didn't understand what he meant. He said that the day before, when I'd been crying and crying, he'd decided that today I wasn't going to cry even once. I didn't understand either how I had become this person who was so easy to hurt. Had I always been this person, or had life worn me down, broken me for good? I remembered myself being less vulnerable before. I'd never run home crying when I fell and hurt myself skipping in the street, or when the older boys I played football with were rough. I could be the toughest of them all, nearly as tough as my best friend. I had to be courageous and make myself vulnerable in love, even if it hurt. The way he looked at me sometimes. I'd been wondering about it – that look he often gave me, as if he was searching for pebbles at the bottom of a deep well.

But when we got home and were brushing our teeth, I realised it was the same look he gave himself when he looked in the mirror.

*

You grow in your sleep, you grow in my arms; it's as if I can feel your back, your fingers, your legs growing longer, your body becoming heavier as I sit here. It's almost night and the lights are going off in the windows of the building opposite. You're nearly five months old. So far you're an unflappable, patient soul; when your brother sings and is silly for us, your wide eyes observe from the sidelines, but when it's you he's being silly for, you laugh and can hardly stop. Your father and I can never make you laugh like that. Even now it's as if I can tell which of you is going to have the easier life in certain respects, the harder in others; even now it's as if you've always been a part of my life. When I think back to my life before, I've got to remember first that the two of you weren't there then; only then can I retrieve the memories. Your lives have coloured them all.

*

What's that noise, is there a door open? my mum asked, and we had to pull in at a bus stop to check. She stepped out, into the driving snow in this eternal winter, and opened and closed all the doors one after another. It was a few days ago and we were on our way to a library event in the depths of the country. My mum was with me to look after you while I was on stage. She's even happier being with you than she is in her kayak, even though that's the best thing she knows; she can do the Eskimo roll both ways in open water.

Illuminated by the main beam the snowflakes looked like long white hair waving and batting at the windscreen. I was sitting in the back and you were asleep in your child seat next to me. I dread driving, even more so since the two of you came along, but my mum drove carefully; she said she'd slept really well that night and felt more rested than usual. Then there was a noise again, slightly louder than before. What's that? she exclaimed. It's the wipers, I said. Oh, so it is, she said, and switched them off. But it was snowing so much she had to switch them on again. I've been meaning to get them changed soon anyway, she said, it makes no odds if we wear these ones out.

My dad kept texting. 'There yet?' he wrote casually, as if unconcerned, then after a while came, 'There yet???', followed shortly after by, '????'.

I've thought that I must write a book about Mum and Dad, because after Edel died they've been left without a buffer in front of them. I dreamt that Edel died, and she did. I know she would have died anyway, but I've got to tell myself the whole time not to think I'm a soothsayer or that I can make things happen by the power of thought alone. For Mum and Dad, death now gapes like a hole in the ice up ahead. I don't like to think about that. If I write about them, it'll stop me thinking about it so much.

One of the last summers when Mum took Edel out to swim in the fjord, Edel had to crawl out on all fours – she couldn't find her balance on the stones and came crawling onto the shore with seaweed in her hair. She looked like Neptune, Mum said, it was a bit humiliating.

I was there too, sitting on a bench by the shore. Mum had driven me, though it was only a ten-minute walk from the cabin to the water, ten minutes down the hill, but I couldn't manage to walk that far. Edel walked, even though she was ninety years old, and I was only twenty-five. I was so ill that summer, all I could do was lie in bed in the cabin. I'd given up my studies, the boy I lived with had broken up with me, life was grime trickling down the window panes. Later, Edel spoke of how worried she was: she was so worried because I'd lost all my strength just at the time I needed to reach out and grasp hold of adulthood; my friends were grasping their own lives with all the vigour and strength that came so naturally to them – graduating, pairing off, heading out for weekends in the fells with bottles of wine in their rucksacks and skis under their arms, before securing good jobs and starting families. Becoming adult is so very much harder when you haven't the strength.

I waved to Edel as she sat getting dressed again on a rock. It takes such a long time to put your knickers and trousers on when you're ninety years old, because it's impossible to stand on one leg. Children played at the water's edge, families gathered underneath parasols and ate their sandwiches, and I didn't know if I'd ever get to have anything like that myself. Edel didn't have children, and I asked her once if she was all right with that. I can't believe I asked her, but if there was anyone I could ask that question it was her. It's all right and it's not, she said. When she was young she didn't want to leave anything behind, didn't want anything of her to remain after she was gone. People leave all sorts of mess, she said, and she didn't want that. But I said it wasn't true, that she was leaving a lot of things – all the talks we'd had, they were all very much still a part of me. Yes, I suppose you're right there, she said. But she'd never thought that she needed a child to make life good. Then she got to the age when it was too late anyway, and she still didn't want children, but she thought about it a lot at that time. My head may not have wanted any, but my body was grieving, she said.

I looked at Edel as she waved back and I thought to myself that my life could be good even if I didn't get to have a family of my own, but I didn't know if it could be good if I kept being ill. So ill that I couldn't walk for ten minutes, couldn't swim in the fjord, if it was going to be like this for ever.

Edel dropped her bathing suit into her bag and I got up off the bench and walked the few metres back to the car. I didn't want her to see I was crying. It wasn't because I was scared. Often I cried because I was scared about the future, but now I lay down on the back seat in the boiling hot car and cried for all the years that had gone by while I was ill, all the years I'd lost.

Driving back from the library, the snow still coming down outside, Mum said to me, The child does the funniest things, like after dinner, when he put his legs up on the table and covered his face with his bib before making snoring-whistling sounds, pretending he was having an after-dinner nap. I think he's funny too. The fact that he's got his own personality continues to surprise me; he was his own person from the minute he arrived. Was I like that? I asked Mum. Did I do things like that? I don't know, she said, I can hardly remember. You did use to put your summer dress on on top of your winter dress, I've told you that, but you might have been bigger then, and then your brothers came along, I lose track. The years you can't remember as a child, your parents can't remember either; why does nature do that, make those early years such a secret? The child is a secret to others, the child is a secret to itself.

I hope Mum and Dad have forgotten when they had a new child in the house too. After my brothers and I had moved out, I came home again, a twenty-five-year-old child they had to cook for. Dad would come home from work to make me an omelette and Mum would read aloud to me from a children's book called *Kjersti*. They were strong for me, full of courage and stamina and endeavour. They never let on how afraid and despairing they must have been, and I remember my mum one time saying that when you're off in the fells in a snowstorm, pulling your child behind you in a pulk, it's no use lying down and giving up. I'm so glad it's my turn to be grown-up now, that I don't have to be the child any more.

*

It's dark outside and I should be sleeping, but I don't dare to. I become convinced that I need to go out.

The fear of night has come over me. It comes with the darkness. I can't talk to Bo, I'm still trying my best not to bother him with my insomnia. *An adult is someone who is able to bear the weight of their own emotional life without faltering and without bothering others with it*, a friend wrote to me. I don't think it was meant personally. I agree up to a point, even if I also think we need to look after each other. I can't put you down on the sofa or the bed – you'll only wake up – so I open the door of the study and give you to Bo. I need to go for a walk, I tell him. What, now? he says. Yes, I say.

Outside, the night isn't nearly so frightening. The moon keeps an eye on me. I even see some stars. I walk along the river in the dark, and I remember then what it's like to be me; at the end of the day I'm just me. I note down words in my mind, words to say to you when we wake up in the morning, but we'll wake up many times before then. I've told you about how your father and I got together, and now you know it's been far from a happy story, the kind I would have wanted to tell you; it's been the opposite, really, but fortunately it's not just happy stories that end well. I can't tell you that much about our being

153

together – that's where your father and I are now, and my view of it changes by the day, the whole time, and besides, what I tell you will always be coloured by a strong hope that we're going to get by. Your father and I keep on running through the glass wall. Over and over again. We take our marks, close our eyes and launch ourselves through the wall, he and I together, side by side, me in front of him, him in front of me, we hold each other's hands. Are we going to make it? he asks, I ask, but we can't ask, we just have to make it. We've got no choice any more. We have to make it through that wall every single time, even if it means cutting ourselves to pieces, even though we're consumed by despair: we just have to keep running through the glass. There's no other option.

I turn back then and start walking home, thinking about something else. My legs move on their own, all the way into the rear courtyard and up the stairs to the third floor, to the red door, and before I notice where I am, I'm home again. Still, it's strange – it feels as though I'm standing outside an unfamiliar place; I can't grasp that this red door is mine, where I live.

*

It's dark inside the flat. There's no one in the kitchen, no one in the living room, no one in the study. I open the bedroom door and there you are, the three of you asleep in the same bed, limbs everywhere. I climb into bed with you and lie there quiet as a mouse. I'm surrounded by sleeping people, people who've come to me and come out of me, whose sounds and smells fill the room, the steady breathing of the child, the sweet smell of you. I've realised that the deepest, most painful unease can seldom be thought away; it's smarter to shift one's thoughts to the body, to gauge how the body is feeling. In these moments it helps to lie down with Bo. I need to feel the warmth from his skin, to hear the rumble of sleep in his chest, because then the unease turns into something else; it dissolves, it disappears.

Notes

p. xx   '*The bird fights its way out of the egg . . .*' Hermann Hesse,
         Demian, trans. Damion Searls, Penguin Classics, 2013

p. xx   '*I've been born again and again . . .*' Agnes Martin, *With My*
         Back to the World, documentary, 2003

p. xx   '*purify his individuality and refine his spirit*' August Strindberg,
         'purify my individuality and refine my spirit', *Inferno*, in
         Inferno and From an Occult Diary, trans. Mary Sandbach,
         Penguin Classics, 1979

p. xx   '*Poetry is not a turning loose of emotion*' T. S. Eliot, 'Tradition
         and the Individual Talent', *The Egoist*, 1919

p. xx   '*Our life is a journey, through winter and night . . .*'
         Louis-Ferdinand Céline, 'Song of the Swiss Guards',
         1793, *Journey to the End of the Night*, trans. Ralph
         Manheim, New Directions, 1983

p. xx   '*Oh why, why must the same love made me laugh make me cry*'
         Bonnie Billy, cover of 'Same Love That Made Me
         Laugh' (Bill Withers), *More Revery*, EP, 2000

p. xx   '*I wake up at night, I see the other side of the world . . .*' Jacques
         Roubaud, 'Transworld (iii)', *Towards a New Poetics:*
         Contemporary Writing in France, trans. Serge Gavronsky,
         University of California Press, 1994

p. xx   '*I have noticed that doing the sensible thing is only a good idea . . .*'
         Jeanette Winterson, *Why Be Happy When You Could Be*
         Normal, Jonathan Cape, 2011

p. xx   '*An adult is someone who is able to bear the weight of their own*
         emotional life . . .' Peter Bastian, *Mesterlære: En Livsfortælling*,
         Gyldendal, Copenhagen, 2012